CR

Ed McBain is one of the most illustrious names in crime fiction. In 1998, he was the first non-British author to be awarded the Crime Writers' Association Cartier Diamond Dagger Award and he is also a holder of the Mystery Writers of America's coveted Grand Master Award. Ed McBain died in 2005. Visit his website at www.edmcbain.com.

GW00320339

59
4

TRANSGRESSIONS

VOLUME 2

Three brand new novellas

STEPHEN KING
WALTER MOSLEY
LAWRENCE BLOCK

Edited by Ed McBain

An Orion paperback

First published in Great Britain in 2005
by Orion
This paperback edition published in 2006
by Orion Books Ltd,
Orion House, 5 Upper St Martin's Lane,
London WC2H 9EA

1 3 5 7 9 10 8 6 4 2

The Things They Left Behind copyright © 2005 by Stephen King
Archibald Lawless, Anarchist at Large: Walking the Line
copyright © 2005 by Walter Mosley
Keller's Adjustment copyright © 2005 by Lawrence Block

TRANSGRESSIONS 2
Copyright © Hui Corp 2005

The right of the authors to be identified as the authors of
this work has been asserted by them in accordance with the
Copyright, Designs and Patents Act 1988.

All rights reserved. No part of this publication may be
reproduced, stored in a retrieval system, or transmitted,
in any form or by any means, electronic, mechanical,
photocopying, recording or otherwise, without the prior
permission of the copyright owner.

All the characters in this book are fictitious, and any
resemblance to actual persons living or dead is
purely coincidental.

A CIP catalogue record for this book
is available from the British Library.

ISBN 13: 978-0-7528-7948-2
ISBN 10: 0-7528-7948-0

Printed in Great Britain by Clays Ltd, St Ives plc

The Orion Publishing Group's policy is to use papers that
are natural, renewable and recyclable products and made
from wood grown in sustainable forests. The logging and
manufacturing processes are expected to conform to the
environmental regulations of the country of origin.

www.orionbooks.co.uk

Contents

Introduction

When I was writing novellas for the pulp magazines back in the 1950s, we still called them "novelettes," and all I knew about the form was that it was long and it paid half a cent a word. This meant that if I wrote 10,000 words, the average length of a novelette back then, I would sooner or later get a check for five hundred dollars. This was not bad pay for a struggling young writer.

A novella today can run anywhere from 10,000 to 40,000 words. Longer than a short story (5,000 words) but much shorter than a novel (at least 60,000 words) it combines the immediacy of the former with the depth of the latter, and it ain't easy to write. In fact, given the difficulty of the form, and the scarcity of markets for novellas, it is surprising that any writers today are writing them at all.

But here was the brilliant idea.

Round up the best writers of mystery, crime, and suspense novels, and ask them to write a brand-new novella for a collection of similarly superb novellas to be published anywhere in the world for the very first time. Does that sound keen, or what? In a perfect world, *yes*, it *is* a wonderful idea, and here is your novella, sir, thank you very much for asking me to contribute.

But many of the bestselling novelists I approached had never written a novella in their lives. (Some of them had never even written a short story!) Up went the hands in mock horror. "What! A novella? I wouldn't even know how to *begin* one." Others thought that writing a novella ("*How* long did you say it had to be?") would constitute a wonderful challenge, but bestselling novelists are busy people with publishing contracts to fulfill and deadlines to meet, and however intriguing the invitation may have seemed at first, stark reality reared its ugly head, and so . . .

"Gee, thanks for thinking of me, but I'm already three months behind deadline," or . . .

"My publisher would *kill* me if I even dreamed of writing something for another house," or . . .

"Try me again a year from now," or . . .

"Have you asked X? Or Y? Or Z?"

What it got down to in the end was a matter of timing and luck. In some cases, a writer I desperately wanted was happily between novels and just happened to have some free time on his/her hands. In other cases, a writer had an idea that was too short for a novel but too long for a short story, so yes, what a wonderful opportunity! In yet other cases, a writer wanted to introduce a new character he or she had been thinking about for some time. In each and every case, the formidable task of writing fiction that fell somewhere between 10,000 and 40,000 words seemed an exciting challenge, and the response was enthusiastic.

Except for length and a loose adherence to crime, mystery, or suspense, I placed no restrictions upon the writers who agreed to contribute. The results are as astonishing as they are brilliant. The ten novellas that follow are as varied as the men and women who concocted them, but they all exhibit the same devoted passion and the same extraordinary writing. More than that, there is an underlying sense here that the writer is attempting something new and unexpected, and willing to share his or her own surprises with us. Just as their names are in alphabetical order on the book jacket, so do their stories follow in reverse alphabetical order: I have no favorites among them. I love them all equally.

Enjoy!

ED MCBAIN
Weston, Connecticut
August 2004

TRANSGRESSIONS

VOLUME 2

STEPHEN KING

There are certain things that are almost always mentioned when the name **Stephen King** comes up. How many books he's sold. What he's doing in and for literature today. One thing almost never mentioned—and not generally perceived—is that he single-handedly made popular fiction grow up. While there were many good bestselling writers before him, King, more than anybody since John D. MacDonald, brought reality to genre novels with his minutely detailed examinations of life and the people of mythical towns in New England that seem to exist due to his amazing talent for making them real in every detail. Of course, combined with the elements of supernatural terror, novels such as *It*, *The Stand*, *Insomnia*, and *Bag of Bones* have propelled him to the top of the bestseller lists time after time. He's often re-marked that *Salem's Lot* was "Peyton Place Meets Dracula." And so it was. The rich characterization, the careful and caring social eye, the interplay of story line and character development announced that writers could take worn themes such as vampirism or ghosts and make them fresh again. Before King, many popular writers found their efforts to make their books serious blue-penciled by their editors. Stuff like that gets in the way of the story, they were told. Well, it's stuff like that that has made King so popular, and helped free the popular name from the shackles of simple genre writing. He is a master of masters. Recently he has been completing his magnum opus fantasy series The Dark Tower, with the last book, *The Dark Tower*, published.

THE THINGS THEY
LEFT BEHIND

Stephen King

The things I want to tell you about—the ones they left behind—
showed up in my apartment in August of 2002. I'm sure of that, because I found most of them not long after I helped Paula Robeson with
her air conditioner. Memory always needs a marker, and that's mine.
She was a children's book illustrator, good-looking (hell, *fine*-looking),
husband in import-export. A man has a way of remembering occasions
when he's actually able to help a good-looking lady in distress (even
one who keeps assuring you she's "very married"); such occasions are
all too few. These days the would-be knight errant usually just makes
matters worse.

She was in the lobby, looking frustrated, when I came down for
an afternoon walk. I said *Hi, howya doin'*, the way you do to other
folks who share your building, and she asked me in an exasperated
tone that stopped just short of querulousness why the super had to
be on vacation *now*. I pointed out that even cowgirls get the blues
and even supers go on vacation; that August, furthermore, was an extremely logical month to take time off. August in New York (and in
Paris, *mon ami*) finds psychoanalysts, trendy artists, and building su-
perintendents mighty thin on the ground.

She didn't smile. I'm not sure she even got the Tom Robbins ref-
erence (obliqueness is the curse of the reading class). She said it

might be true about August being a good month to take off and go to the Cape or Fire Island, but her damned apartment was just about burning *up* and the damned air conditioner wouldn't so much as burp. I asked her if she'd like me to take a look, and I remember the glance she gave me—those cool, assessing gray eyes. I remember thinking that eyes like that probably saw quite a lot. And I remember smiling at what she asked me: *Are you safe?* It reminded me of that movie, not *Lolita* (thinking about *Lolita*, sometimes at two in the morning, came later) but the one where Laurence Olivier does the impromptu dental work on Dustin Hoffman, asking him over and over again, *Is it safe?*

I'm safe, I said. *Haven't attacked a woman in over a year. I used to attack two or three a week, but the meetings are helping.*

A giddy thing to say, but I was in a fairly giddy mood. A *summer* mood. She gave me another look, and then *she* smiled. Put out her hand. *Paula Robeson,* she said. It was the left hand she put out—not normal, but the one with the plain gold band on it. I think that was probably on purpose, don't you? But it was later that she told me about her husband being in import-export. On the day when it was my turn to ask *her* for help.

In the elevator, I told her not to expect too much. Now, if she'd wanted a man to find out the underlying causes of the New York City Draft Riots, or to supply a few amusing anecdotes about the creation of the smallpox vaccine, or even to dig up quotes on the sociological ramifications of the TV remote control (the most important invention of the last fifty years, in my 'umble opinion), I was the guy.

Research is your game, Mr. Staley? she asked as we went up in the slow and clattery elevator.

I admitted that it was, although I didn't add that I was still quite new to it. Nor did I ask her to call me Scott—that would have spooked her all over again. And I certainly didn't tell her that I was trying to forget all I'd once known about rural insurance. That I was, in fact, trying to forget quite a lot of things, including about two dozen faces.

You see, I may be trying to forget, but I still remember quite a lot. I think we all do, when we put our minds to it (and sometimes, rather more nastily, when we don't). I even remember something one of those South American novelists said—you know, the ones they call the Magical Realists? Not the guy's name, that's not important, but this quote: *As infants, our first victory comes in grasping some bit of the world, usually our mothers' fingers. Later we discover that the world, and the things of the world, are grasping us, and have been, all along.* Borges? Yes, it might have been Borges. Or it might have been Remarquez. That I *don't* remember. I just know I got her air conditioner running, and when cool air started blowing out of the convector, it lit up her whole face. I also know it's true, that thing about how perception switches around and we come to realize that the things we thought we were holding are actually holding us. Keeping us prisoner, perhaps—Thoreau certainly thought so—but also holding us in place. That's the trade-off. And no matter what Thoreau might have thought, I believe the trade is mostly a fair one. Or I did then; now, I'm not so sure.

And I know these things happened in late August of 2002, not quite a year after a piece of the sky fell down and everything changed for all of us.

On an afternoon about a week after Sir Scott Staley donned his Good Samaritan armor and successfully battled the fearsome air conditioner, I took my afternoon walk to the Staples on Eighty-third Street to get a box of Zip discs and a ream of paper. I owed a fellow forty pages of background on the development of the Polaroid camera (which is more interesting a story as you might think). When I got back to my apartment, there was a pair of sunglasses with red frames and very distinctive lenses on the little table in the foyer where I keep bills that need to be paid, claim checks, overdue-book notices, and things of that nature. I recognized the glasses at once, and all the strength went out of me. I didn't fall, but I dropped my packages on the floor and leaned against the side of the door, trying to catch my breath and staring at those sunglasses. If there had been nothing to lean against, I believe I would have swooned like a miss in a Victorian novel—one of those where the lustful vampire appears at the stroke of midnight.

Two related but distinct emotional waves struck me. The first was that sense of horrified shame you feel when you know you're about to be caught in some act you will never be able to explain. The memory that comes to mind in this regard is of a thing that happened to me—or almost happened—when I was sixteen.

My mother and sister had gone shopping in Portland and I supposedly had the house to myself until evening. I was reclining naked on my bed with a pair of my sister's underpants wrapped around my cock. The bed was scattered with pictures I'd clipped from magazines I'd found in the back of the garage—the previous owner's stash of *Penthouse* and *Gallery* magazines, very likely. I heard a car come crunching into the driveway. No mistaking the sound of that motor; it was my mother and sister. Peg had come down with some sort of flu bug and started vomiting out the window. They'd gotten as far as Poland Springs and turned around.

I looked at the pictures scattered all over the bed, my clothes scattered all over the floor, and the foam of pink rayon in my left hand. I remember how the strength flowed out of my body, and the terrible sense of lassitude that came in its place. My mother was yelling for me—"Scott, Scott, come down and help me with your sister, she's sick"—and I remember thinking, "What's the use? I'm caught. I might as well accept it, I'm caught and this is the first thing they'll think of when they think about me for the rest of my life: Scott, the jerk-off artist."

But more often than not a kind of survival overdrive kicks in at such moments. That's what happened to me. I might go down, I decided, but I wouldn't do so without at least an effort to save my dignity. I threw the pictures and the panties under the bed. Then I jumped into my clothes, moving with numb but sure-fingered speed, all the time thinking of this crazy old game-show I used to watch, *Beat the Clock*.

I can remember how my mother touched my flushed cheek when I got downstairs, and the thoughtful concern in her eyes. "Maybe you're getting sick, too," she said.

"Maybe I am," I said, and gladly enough. It was half an hour before I discovered I'd forgotten to zip my fly. Luckily, neither Peg nor my mother noticed, although on any other occasion one or both of them would have asked me if I had a license to sell hot dogs (this was what passed for wit in the house where I grew up). That day one of them was too sick and the other was too worried to be witty. So I got a total pass.

Lucky me.

What followed the first emotional wave that August day in my apartment was much simpler: I thought I was going out of my mind. Because those glasses couldn't be there. Absolutely could. Not. No way.

Then I raised my eyes and saw something else that had most certainly not been in my apartment when I left for Staples half an hour before (locking the door behind me, as I always did). Leaning in the corner between the kitchenette and the living room was a baseball bat. Hillerich & Bradsby, according to the label. And while I couldn't see the other side, I knew what was printed there well enough: CLAIMS ADJUSTOR, the words burned into the ash with the tip of a soldering iron and then colored deep blue.

Another sensation rushed through me: a third wave. This was a species of surreal dismay. I don't believe in ghosts, but I'm sure that at that moment I looked as though I had just seen one.

I felt that way, too. Yes indeed. Because those sunglasses had to be gone—long-time gone, as the Dixie Chicks say. Ditto Cleve Farrell's Claims Adjustor. ("Besboll been bery-bery good to mee," Cleve would sometimes say, waving the bat over his head as he sat at his desk. "In-SHOO-rance been bery-bery bad.")

I did the only thing I could think of, which was to grab up Sonja D'Amico's shades and trot back down to the elevator with them, holding them out in front of me the way you might hold out something nasty you found on your apartment floor after a week away on vacation—a piece of decaying food, or the body of a poisoned mouse. I found myself remembering a conversation I'd had about Sonja with a fellow named Warren Anderson. *She must have looked like she thought she was going to pop back up and ask somebody for a Coca-Cola*, I had thought when he told me what he'd seen. Over drinks in the Blarney Stone Pub on Third Avenue, this had been, about six weeks after the sky fell down. After we'd toasted each other on not being dead.

Things like that have a way of sticking, whether you want them to or not. Like a musical phrase or the nonsense chorus to a pop song that you just can't get out of your head. You wake up at three in the morning, needing to take a leak, and as you stand there in front of the bowl, your cock in your hand and your mind about ten per cent awake, it comes back to you: *Like she thought she was going to pop back up. Pop back up and ask for a Coke.* At some point during that conversation Warren had asked me if I remembered her funny sunglasses, and I said I did. Sure I did.

Four floors down, Pedro the doorman was standing in the shade of the awning and talking with Rafe the FedEx man. Pedro was a serious hardboy when it came to letting deliverymen stand in front of the building—he had a seven-minute rule, a pocket watch with which to enforce it, and all the beat cops were his buddies—but he got on with Rafe, and sometimes the two of them would stand there for twenty minutes or more with their heads together, doing the old New York Yak. Politics? Besboll? The Gospel According to Henry David Thoreau? I didn't know and never cared less than on that day. They'd been there when I went up with my office supplies, and were still there when a far less carefree Scott Staley came back down. A Scott Staley who had discovered a small but noticeable hole in the column of reality. Just the two of them being there was enough for me. I walked up and held my right hand, the one with the sunglasses in it, out to Pedro.

"What would you call these?" I asked, not bothering to excuse myself or anything, just butting in head-first.

He gave me a considering stare that said, "I am surprised at your rudeness, Mr. Staley, truly I am," then looked down at my hand. For a long moment he said nothing, and a horrible idea took possession of me: he saw nothing because there was nothing to see. Only my hand outstretched, as if this were Turnabout Tuesday and I expected *him* to tip *me*. My hand was empty. Sure it was, had to be, because Sonja D'Amico's sunglasses no longer existed. Sonja's joke shades were a long time gone.

"I call them sunglasses, Mr. Staley," Pedro said at last. "What else would I call them? Or is this some sort of trick question?"

Rafe the FedEx man, clearly more interested, took them from me. The relief of seeing him holding the sunglasses and looking at them, almost *studying* them, was like having someone scratch that exact place between your shoulder blades that itches. He stepped out from beneath the awning and held them up to the day, making a sunstar flash off each of the heart-shaped lenses.

"They're like the ones the little girl wore in that porno movie with Jeremy Irons," he said at last.

I had to grin in spite of my distress. In New York, even the deliverymen are film critics. It's one of the things to love about the place.

"That's right, *Lolita*," I said, taking the glasses back. "Only the heart-shaped sunglasses were in the version Stanley Kubrick directed. Back when Jeremy Irons was still nothing but a putter." That one hardly made sense (even to me), but I didn't give Shit One. Once again I was feeling giddy . . . but not in a good way. Not this time.

"Who played the pervo in that one?" Rafe asked.

I shook my head. "I'll be damned if I can remember right now."

"If you don't mind me saying," Pedro said, "you look rather pale, Mr. Staley. Are you coming down with something? The flu, perhaps?"

No, that was my sister, I thought of saying. *The day I came within about twenty seconds of getting caught masturbating into her panties while I looked at a picture of Miss April.* But I hadn't been caught. Not then, not on 9/11, either. Fooled ya, beat the clock again. I couldn't speak for Warren Anderson, who told me in the Blarney Stone that he'd stopped on the third floor that morning to talk about the Yankees with a friend, but not getting caught had become quite a specialty of mine.

"I'm all right," I told Pedro, and while that wasn't true, knowing I wasn't the only one who saw Sonja's joke shades as a thing that actually existed in the world made me feel better, at least. If the sunglasses were in the world, probably Cleve Farrell's Hillerich & Bradsby was, too.

"Are those *the* glasses?" Rafe suddenly asked in a respectful, ready-to-be-awestruck voice. "The ones from the first *Lolita*?"

"Nope," I said, folding the bows behind the heart-shaped lenses, and as I did, the name of the girl in the Kubrick version of the film came to me: Sue Lyon. I still couldn't remember who played the pervo. "Just a knock-off."

"Is there something special about them?" Rafe asked. "Is that why you came rushing down here?"

"I don't know," I said. "Someone left them behind in my apartment."

I went upstairs before they could ask any more questions and looked around, hoping there was nothing else. But there was. In addition to the sunglasses and the baseball bat with CLAIMS ADJUSTOR burned into the side, there was a Howie's Laff-Riot Farting Cushion, a conch shell, a steel penny suspended in a Lucite cube, and a ceramic mushroom (red with white spots) that came with a ceramic Alice sitting on top of it. The Farting Cushion had belonged to Jimmy

Eagleton and got a certain amount of play every year at the Christmas party. The ceramic Alice had been on Maureen Hannon's desk—a gift from her granddaughter, she'd told me once. Maureen had the most beautiful white hair, which she wore long, to her waist. You rarely see that in a business situation, but she'd been with the company for almost forty years and felt she could wear her hair any way she liked. I remembered both the conch shell and the steel penny, but not in whose cubicles (or offices) they had been. It might come to me; it might not. There had been lots of cubicles (and offices) at Light and Bell, Insurers.

The shell, the mushroom, and the Lucite cube were on the coffee table in my living room, gathered in a neat pile. The Farting Cushion was—quite rightly, I thought—lying on top of my toilet tank, beside the current issue of Spenck's Rural Insurance Newsletter. Rural insurance used to be my specialty, as I think I told you. I knew all the odds.

What were the odds on this?

When something goes wrong in your life and you need to talk about it, I think that the first impulse for most people is to call a family member. This wasn't much of an option for me. My father put an egg in his shoe and beat it when I was two and my sister was four. My mother, no quitter she, hit the ground running and raised the two of us, managing a mail-order clearinghouse out of our home while she did so. I believe this was a business she actually created, and she made an adequate living at it (only the first year was really scary, she told me later). She smoked like a chimney, however, and died of lung cancer at the age of forty-eight, six or eight years before the Internet might have made her a dot-com millionaire.

My sister Peg was currently living in Cleveland, where she had embraced Mary Kay Cosmetics, the Indians, and fundamentalist Christianity, not necessarily in that order. If I called and told Peg about the things I'd found in my apartment, she would suggest I get down on my knees and ask Jesus to come into my life. Rightly or wrongly, I did not feel Jesus could help me with my current problem.

I was equipped with the standard number of aunts, uncles, and cousins, but most lived west of the Mississippi, and I hadn't seen any of them in years. The Killians (my mother's side of the family) have never been a reuning bunch. A card on one's birthday and at Christmas were considered sufficient to fulfill all familial obligations. A card on Valentine's Day or at Easter was a bonus. I called my sister on Christmas or she called me, we muttered the standard crap about getting together "sometime soon," and hung up with what I imagine was mutual relief.

The next option when in trouble would probably be to invite a good friend out for a drink, explain the situation, and then ask for advice. But I was a shy boy who grew into a shy man, and in my current research job I work alone (out of preference) and thus have no colleagues apt to mature into friends. I made a few in my last job— Sonja and Cleve Farrell, to name two—but they're dead, of course.

I reasoned that if you don't have a friend you can talk to, the next-best thing would be to rent one. I could certainly afford a little therapy, and it seemed to me that a few sessions on some psychiatrist's couch (four might do the trick) would be enough for me to explain what had happened and to articulate how it made me feel. How much could four sessions set me back? Six hundred dollars? Maybe eight? That seemed a fair price for a little relief. And I thought there might be a bonus. A disinterested outsider might be able to see some simple and reasonable explanation I was just missing. To my mind the locked door between my apartment and the outside world seemed to do away with most of those, but it was *my* mind, after all; wasn't that the point? And perhaps the problem?

I had it all mapped out. During the first session I'd explain what had happened. When I came to the second one, I'd bring the items in question—sunglasses, Lucite cube, conch shell, baseball bat, ceramic mushroom, the ever-popular Farting Cushion. A little show and tell, just like in grammar school. That left two more during which my rent-a-pal and I could figure out the cause of this disturbing tilt in the axis of my life and set things straight again.

A single afternoon spent riffling the Yellow Pages and dialing the telephone was enough to prove to me that the idea of psychiatry was unworkable in fact, no matter how good it might be in theory. The closest I came to an actual appointment was a receptionist who told me that Dr. Jauss might be able to work me in the following January. She intimated even that would take some inspired shoehorning. The others held out no hope whatsoever. I tried half a dozen therapists in Newark and four in White Plains, even a hypnotist in Queens, with the same result. Mohammed Atta and his Suicide Patrol might have been very bery-bery bad for the city of New York (not to mention for the in-SHOO-rance business), but it was clear to me from that single fruitless afternoon on the telephone that they had been a boon to the psychiatric profession, much as the psychiatrists themselves might wish otherwise. If you wanted to lie on some professional's couch in the summer of 2002, you had to take a number and wait in line.

I could sleep with those things in my apartment, but not well. They whispered to me. I lay awake in my bed, sometimes until two, thinking about Maureen Hannon, who felt she had reached an age (not to mention a level of indispensability) at which she could wear her amazingly long hair any way she damn well liked. Or I'd recall the various people who'd gone running around at the Christmas party, waving Jimmy Eagleton's famous Farting Cushion. It was, as I may have said, a great favorite once people got two or three drinks closer to New Year's. I remembered Bruce Mason asking me if it didn't look like an enema bag for elfs—"elfs," he said—and by a process of association remembered that the conch shell had been his. Of course. Bruce Mason, Lord of the Flies. And a step further down the associative food-chain I found the name and face of James Mason, who had played Humbert Humbert back when Jeremy Irons was still just a putter. The mind is a wily monkey; sometime him take-a de banana, sometime him don't. Which is why I'd brought the sunglasses downstairs, although I'd been aware of no deductive process at the time. I'd only wanted confirmation. There's a George Seferis poem that asks, *Are these the voices of our dead friends, or is it just the gramophone?* Sometimes it's a good question, one you have to ask someone else. Or . . . listen to this.

Once, in the late eighties, near the end of a bitter two-year romance with alcohol, I woke up in my study after dozing off at my desk in the middle of the night. I staggered off to my bedroom, where, as I reached for the light switch, I saw someone moving around. I flashed on the idea (the near *certainty*) of a junkie burglar with a cheap pawnshop .32 in his trembling hand, and my heart almost came out of my chest. I turned on the light with one hand and was grabbing for something heavy off the top of my bureau with the other—anything, even the silver frame holding the picture of my mother, would have done—when I saw the prowler was me. I was staring wild-eyed back at myself from the mirror on the other side of the room, my shirt half-untucked and my hair standing up in the back. I was disgusted with myself, but I was also relieved.

I wanted this to be like that. I wanted it to be the mirror, the gramophone, even someone playing a nasty practical joke (maybe someone who knew why I hadn't been at the office on that day in September). But I knew it was none of those things. The Farting Cushion was there, an actual guest in my apartment. I could run my thumb over the buckles on Alice's ceramic shoes, slide my finger down the part in her yellow ceramic hair. I could read the date on the penny inside the Lucite cube.

Bruce Mason, alias Conch Man, alias Lord of the Flies, took his big pink shell to the company shindig at Jones Beach one July and blew it, summoning people to a jolly picnic lunch of hotdogs and hamburgers. Then he tried to show Freddy Lounds how to do it. The best Freddy had been able to muster was a series of weak honk-ing sounds like . . . well, like Jimmy Eagleton's Farting Cushion. Around and around it goes. Ultimately, every associative chain forms a necklace.

In late September I had a brainstorm, one of those ideas so simple you can't believe you didn't think of it sooner. Why was I was hold-ing onto this unwelcome crap, anyway? Why not just get rid of it? It wasn't as if the items were in trust; the people who owned them weren't going to come back at some later date and ask for them to be returned. The last time I'd seen Cleve Farrell's face it had been on a poster, and the last of those had been torn down by November of '01. The general (if unspoken) feeling was that such homemade homages were bumming out the tourists, who'd begun to creep back to Fun City. What had happened was horrible, most New Yorkers opined, but America was still here and Matthew Broderick would only be in *The Producers* for so long.

I'd gotten Chinese that night, from a place I like two blocks over. My plan was to eat it as I usually ate my evening meal, watching Chuck Scarborough explain the world to me. I was turning on the television when the epiphany came. They *weren't* in trust, these unwelcome souvenirs of the last safe day, nor were they evidence. There had been a crime, yes—everyone agreed to that—but the perpetrators were dead and the ones who'd set them on their crazy course were on the run. There might be trials at some future date, but Scott Staley would never be called to the stand, and Jimmy Eagleton's Farting Cushion would never be marked Exhibit A.

I left my General Tso's chicken sitting on the kitchen counter with the cover still on the aluminum dish, got a laundry bag from the shelf above my seldom-used washing machine, put the things into it (sacking them up, I couldn't believe how light they were, or how long I'd waited to do such a simple thing), and rode down in the elevator with the bag sitting between my feet. I walked to the corner of 75th and Park, looked around to make sure I wasn't being watched (God knows why I felt so furtive, but I did), then put litter in its place. I took one look back over my shoulder as I walked away. The handle of the bat poked out of the basket invitingly. Someone would come along and take it, I had no doubt. Probably before Chuck Scarborough gave way to John Seigenthaler or whoever else was sitting in for Tom Brokaw that evening.

On my way back to my apartment, I stopped at Fun Choy for a fresh order of General Tso's. "Last one no good?" asked Rose Ming, at the cash register. She spoke with some concern. "You tell why."

"No, the last one was fine," I said. "Tonight I just felt like two."

She laughed as though this were the funniest thing she'd ever heard, and I laughed, too. Hard. The kind of laughter that goes well beyond giddy. I couldn't remember the last time I'd laughed like that, so loudly and so naturally. Certainly not since Light and Bell, Insurers, fell into West Street.

I rode the elevator up to my floor and walked the twelve steps to 4-B. I felt the way seriously ill people must when they awaken one day, assess themselves by the sane light of morning, and discover that the fever has broken. I tucked my takeout bag under my left arm (an awkward maneuver but workable in the short run) and then unlocked my door. I turned on the light. There, on the table where I leave bills that need to be paid, claim checks, and overdue-book notices, were Sonja D'Amico's joke sunglasses, the ones with the red frames and the heart-shaped Lolita lenses. Sonja D'Amico who had, according to Warren Anderson (who was, so far as I knew, the only other surviving employee of Light and Bell's home office), jumped from the one hundred and tenth floor of the stricken building.

He claimed to have seen a photo that caught her as she dropped, Sonja with her hands placed primly on her skirt to keep it from skating up her thighs, her hair standing up against the smoke and blue of that day's sky, the tips of her shoes pointed down. The description made me think of "Falling," the poem James Dickey wrote about the stewardess who tries to aim the plummeting stone of her body for water, as if she could come up smiling, shaking beads of water from her hair and asking for a Coca-Cola.

"I vomited," Warren told me that day in the Blarney Stone. "I never want to look at a picture like that again, Scott, but I know I'll never forget it. You could see her face, and I think she believed that somehow . . . yeah, that somehow she was going to be all right."

I've never screamed as an adult, but I almost did so when I looked from Sonja's sunglasses to Cleve Farrell's CLAIMS ADJUSTOR, the latter once more leaning nonchalantly in the corner by the entry to the living room. Some part of my mind must have remembered that the door to the hallway was open and both of my fourth-floor neighbors would hear me if I did scream; then, as the saying is, I would have some 'splainin to do.

I clapped my hand over my mouth to hold it in. The bag with the General Tso's chicken inside fell to the hardwood floor of the foyer and split open. I could barely bring myself to look at the resulting mess. Those dark chunks of cooked meat could have been anything.

I plopped into the single chair I keep in the foyer and put my face in my hands. I didn't scream and I didn't cry, and after a while I was able to clean up the mess. My mind kept trying to go toward the things that had beaten me back from the corner of 75th and Park, but I wouldn't let it. Each time it tried to lunge in that direction, I grabbed its leash and forced it away again.

That night, lying in bed, I listened to conversations. First the things talked (in low voices), and then the people who had owned the things replied (in slightly louder ones). Sometimes they talked about the picnic at Jones Beach—the coconut odor of suntan lotion and Lou Bega singing "Mambo Number Five" over and over from Misha Bryzinski's boom box. Or they talked about Frisbees sailing under the sky while dogs chased them. Sometimes they discussed children puddling along the wet sand with the seats of their shorts and their bathing suits sagging. Mothers in swimsuits ordered from the Land's End catalogue walking beside them with white gloop on their noses. How many of the kids that day had lost a guardian Mom or a Frisbee-throwing Dad? Man, that was a math problem I didn't want to do. But the voices I heard in my apartment *did* want do it. They did it over and over.

I remembered Bruce Mason blowing his conch shell and proclaiming himself the Lord of the Flies. I remembered Maureen Hannon once telling me (not at Jones Beach, not this conversation) that *Alice in Wonderland* was the first psychedelic novel. Jimmy Eagleton telling me one afternoon that his son had a learning disability to go along with his stutter, two for the price of one, and the kid was going to need a tutor in math and another one in French if he was going to get out of high school in the foreseeable future. "Before he's eligible for the AARP discount on textbooks" was how Jimmy had put it. His cheeks pale and a bit stubbly in the long afternoon light, as if that morning the razor had been dull.

I'd been drifting toward sleep, but this last one brought me fully awake again with a start, because I realized the conversation must have taken place not long before September Eleventh. Maybe only days. Perhaps even the Friday before, which would make it the last day I'd ever seen Jimmy alive. And the l'il putter with the stutter and the learning disability: had his name actually been Jeremy, as in Jeremy Irons? Surely not, surely that was just my mind (sometimes him take-a de banana) playing its little games, but it had been *close* to that, by God. Jason, maybe. Or Justin. In the wee hours everything grows, and I remember thinking that if the kid's name *did* turn out to be Jeremy, I'd probably go crazy. Straw that broke the camel's back, baby.

Around three in the morning I remembered who had owned the Lucite cube with the steel penny in it: Roland Abelson, in Liability. He called it his retirement fund. It was Roland who had a habit of saying "Lucy, you got some 'splainin to do." One night in the fall of '01, I had seen his widow on the six o'clock news. I had talked with her at one of the company picnics (very likely the one at Jones Beach) and thought then that she was pretty, but widowhood had refined that prettiness, winnowed it into severe beauty. On the news report she kept referring to her husband as "missing." She would not call him "dead." And if he *was* alive—if he ever turned up—he would have some 'splainin to do. You bet. But of course, so would she. A woman who has gone from pretty to beautiful as the result of a mass murder would certainly have some 'splainin to do.

Lying in bed and thinking of this stuff—remembering the crash of the surf at Jones Beach and the Frisbees flying under the sky— filled me with an awful sadness that finally emptied in tears. But I have to admit it was a learning experience. That was the night I came to understand that *things*—even little ones, like a penny in a Lucite cube—can get heavier as time passes. But because it's a weight of the mind, there's no mathematical formula for it, like the ones you can find in an insurance company's Blue Books, where the rate on your whole life policy goes up x if you smoke and coverage on your crops goes up y if your farm's in a tornado zone. You see what I'm saying?

It's a weight of the mind.

The following morning I gathered up all the items again, and found a seventh, this one under the couch. The guy in the cubicle next to mine, Misha Bryzinski, had kept a small pair of Punch and Judy dolls on his desk. The one I spied under my sofa with my little eye was Punch. Judy was nowhere to be found, but Punch was enough for me. Those black eyes, staring out from amid the ghost-bunnies, gave me a terrible sinking feeling of dismay. I fished the doll out, hating the streak of dust it left behind. A thing that leaves a trail is a real thing, a thing with weight. No question about it.

I put Punch and all the other stuff in the little utility closet just off the kitchenette, and there they stayed. At first I wasn't sure they would, but they did.

My mother once told me that if a man wiped his ass and saw blood on the toilet tissue, his response would be to shit in the dark for the next thirty days and hope for the best. She used this example to il- lustrate her belief that the cornerstone of male philosophy was "If you ignore it, maybe it'll go away."

I ignored the things I'd found in my apartment, I hoped for the best, and things actually got a little better. I rarely heard those voices whispering in the utility closet (except late at night), although I was more and more apt to take my research chores out of the house. By the middle of November, I was spending most of my days in the New York Public Library. I'm sure the lions got used to seeing me there with my PowerBook.

Then, just before Thanksgiving, I happened to be going out of my building one day and met Paula Robeson, the maiden fair whom I'd rescued by pushing the reset button on her air conditioner, coming in.

With absolutely no forethought whatsoever—if I'd had time to think about it, I'm convinced I never would have said a word—I asked her if I could buy her lunch and talk to her about something.

"The fact is," I said, "I have a problem. Maybe you could push my reset button."

We were in the lobby. Pedro the doorman was sitting in the corner, reading the *Post* (and listening to every word, I have no doubt—to Pedro, his tenants were the world's most interesting daytime drama). She gave me a smile both pleasant and nervous. "I guess I owe you one," she said, "but . . . you know I'm married, don't you?"

"Yes," I said, not adding that she'd shaken with me wrong-handed so I could hardly fail to notice the ring.

She nodded. "Sure, you must've seen us together at least a couple of times, but he was in Europe when I had all that trouble with the air conditioner, and he's in Europe now. Edward, that's his name. Over the last two years he's been in Europe more than he's here, and although I don't like it, I'm very married in spite of it." Then, as a kind of afterthought, she added: "Edward is in import-export."

I used to be in insurance, but then one day the company exploded, I thought of saying. Came *close* to saying, actually. In the end, I managed something a little more sane.

"I don't want a date, Ms. Robeson," No more than I wanted to be on a first-name basis with her, and was that a wink of disappointment I saw in her eyes? By God, I thought it was. But at least it convinced her. I was still *safe*.

She put her hands on her hips and looked at me with mock exasperation. Or maybe not so mock. "Then what *do* you want?"

"Just someone to talk to. I tried several shrinks, but they're . . . busy."

"*All* of them?"

"It would appear so."

"If you're having problems with your sex life or feeling the urge to race around town killing men in turbans, I don't want to know about it."

"It's nothing like that. I'm not going to make you blush, I promise." Which wasn't quite the same as saying *I promise not to shock you* or *You won't think I'm crazy*. "Just lunch and a little advice, that's all I'm asking. What do you say?"

I was surprised—almost flabbergasted—by my own persuasiveness. If I'd planned the conversation in advance, I almost certainly would have blown the whole deal. I suppose she was curious, and I'm sure she heard a degree of sincerity in my voice. She may also have surmised that if I was the sort of man who liked to try his hand picking up women, I would have had a go on that day in August when I'd actually been alone with her in her apartment, the elusive Edward in France or Germany. And I have to wonder how much actual desperation she saw in my face.

In any case, she agreed to have lunch with me at Donald's Grill down the street on Friday. Donald's may be the least romantic restaurant in all of Manhattan—good food, fluorescent lights, waiters who make it clear they'd like you to hurry. She did so with the air of a woman paying an overdue debt about which she's nearly forgotten. This was not exactly flattering, but it was good enough for me. Noon would be fine for her, she said. If I'd meet her in the lobby, we could walk down there together. I told her that would be fine for me, too.

That night was a good one for me. I went to sleep almost immediately, and there were no dreams of Sonja D'Amico going down beside the burning building with her hands on her thighs, like a stewardess looking for water.

As we strolled down 86th Street the following day, I asked Paula where she'd been when she heard.

"San Francisco," she said. "Fast asleep in a Wradling Hotel suite with Edward beside me, undoubtedly snoring as usual. I was coming back here on September twelfth and Edward was going on to Los Angeles for meetings. The hotel management actually rang the fire alarm."

"That must have scared the hell out of you."

"It did, although my first thought wasn't fire but earthquake. Then this disembodied voice came through the speakers, telling us that there was no fire in the hotel, but a hell of a big one in New York."

"Jesus."

"Hearing it like that, in bed in a strange room . . . hearing it come down from the ceiling like the voice of God . . ." She shook her head. Her lips were pressed so tightly together that her lipstick almost disappeared. "That was very frightening. I suppose I understand the urge to pass on news like that, and immediately, but I still haven't entirely forgiven the management of the Wradling for doing it that way. I don't think I'll be staying there again."

"Did your husband go on to his meetings?"

"They were canceled. I imagine a lot of meetings were canceled that day. We stayed in bed with the TV on until the sun came up, trying to get our heads around it. Do you know what I mean?"

"Yes."

"We talked about who might have been there that we knew. I suppose we weren't the only ones doing that, either."

"Did you come up with anyone?"

"A broker from Shearson, Lehman and the assistant manager of the Borders book store in the mall," she said. "One of them was all right. One of them . . . well, you know, one of them wasn't. What about you?"

So I didn't have to sneak up on it, after all. We weren't even at the restaurant yet and here it was.

"*I* would have been there," I said. "I *should* have been there. It's where I worked. In an insurance company on the hundred and tenth floor."

She stopped dead on the sidewalk, looking up at me, eyes wide. I suppose to the people who had to veer around us, we must have looked like lovers. "Scott, *no!*"

"Scott, yes," I said. And finally told someone about how I woke up on September eleventh expecting to do all the things I usually did on weekdays, from the cup of black coffee while I shaved all the way to the cup of cocoa in front of the midnight news summary on Channel Thirteen. A day like any other day, that was what I had in mind. I think that is what Americans had come to expect as their right. Well, guess what? That's an airplane! Flying into the side of a skyscraper! Ha-ha, asshole, the joke's on you, and half the goddam world's laughing!

I told her about looking out my apartment window and seeing the seven A.M. sky was perfectly cloudless, the sort of blue so deep you think you can almost see through it to the stars beyond. Then I told her about the voice. I think everyone has various voices in their heads and we get used to them. When I was sixteen, one of mine spoke up and suggested it might be quite a kick to masturbate into a pair of my sister's underpants. *She has about a thousand pairs and surely won't miss one, y'all*, the voice opined. (I did not tell Paula Robeson about this particular adolescent adventure.) I'd have to call that the voice of utter irresponsibility, more familiarly known as Mr. Yow, Git Down.

"Mr. Yow, Git Down?" Paula asked doubtfully.

"In honor of James Brown, the King of Soul."

"If you say so."

Mr. Yow, Git Down had had less and less to say to me, especially since I'd pretty much given up drinking, and on that day he awoke from his doze just long enough to speak a dozen words, but they were life-changers. Life-*savers*.

The first five (that's me, sitting on the edge of the bed): *Yow, call in sick, y'all!* The next seven (that's me, plodding toward the shower and scratching my left buttock as I go): *Yow, spend the day in Central Park!* There was no premonition involved. It was clearly Mr. Yow, Git Down, not the voice of God. It was just a version of my very own voice (as they all are), in other words, telling me to play hooky. *Do a little suffin fo' yo'self, Gre't God!* The last time I could recall hearing this version of my voice, the subject had been a karaoke contest at a bar on Amersterdam Avenue: *Yow, sing along wit' Neil Diamond, fool— git up on stage and git ya bad self down!*

"I guess I know what you mean," she said, smiling a little.

"Do you?"

"Well . . . I once took off my shirt in a Key West bar and won ten dollars dancing to 'Honky-Tonk Women.'" She paused. "Edward doesn't know, and if you ever tell him, I'll be forced to stab you in the eye with one of his tie tacks."

"Yow, you go, girl," I said, and her smile became a rather wistful grin. It made her look younger. I thought this had a chance of working.

We walked into Donald's. There was a cardboard turkey on the door, cardboard Pilgrims on the green tile wall above the steam table.

"I listened to Mr. Yow, Git Down and I'm here," I said. "But some other things are here, too, and he can't help with them. They're things I can't seem to get rid of. Those are what I want to talk to you about."

"Let me repeat that I'm no shrink," she said, and with more than a trace of uneasiness. The grin was gone. "I majored in German and minored in European history."

You and your husband must have a lot to talk about, I thought. What I said out loud was that it didn't have to be her, necessarily, just someone.

"All right. Just as long as you know."

A waiter took our drink orders, decaf for her, regular for me. Once he went away she asked me what things I was talking about.

"This is one of them." From my pocket I withdrew the Lucite cube with the steel penny suspended inside it and put it on the table. Then I told her about the other things, and to whom they had belonged. Cleve "Besboll been bery-bery good to me" Farrell. Maureen Hannon, who wore her hair long to her waist as a sign of her corporate indispensability. Jimmy Eagleton, who had a divine nose for phony accident claims, a son with learning disabilities, and a Farting Cushion he kept safely tucked away in his desk until the Christmas party rolled around each year. Sonja D'Amico, Light and Bell's best accountant, who had gotten the Lolita sunglasses as a bitter divorce present from her first husband. Bruce "Lord of the Flies" Mason, who would always stand shirtless in my mind's eye, blowing his conch on Jones Beach while the waves rolled up and expired around his bare feet. Last of all, Misha Bryzinski, with whom I'd gone to at least a dozen Mets games. I told her about putting everything but Misha's Punch doll in a trash basket on the corner of Park and 75th, and how they had beaten me back to my apartment, possibly because I had stopped for a second order of General Tso's chicken. During all of this, the Lucite cube stood on the table between us. We managed to eat at least some of our meal in spite of his stern profile.

When I was finished talking, I felt better than I'd dared to hope. But there was a silence from her side of the table that felt terribly heavy.

"So," I said, to break it. "What do you think?"

She took a moment to consider that, and I didn't blame her. "I think that we're not the strangers we were," she said finally, "and making a new friend is never a bad thing. I think I'm glad I know about Mr. Yow, Git Down and that I told you what I did."

"I am, too." And it was true.

"Now may I ask you two questions?"

"Of course."

"How much of what they call 'survivor guilt' are you feeling?"

"I thought you said you weren't a shrink."

"I'm not, but I read the magazines and have even been known to watch *Oprah*. That my husband *does* know, although I prefer not to rub his nose in it. So . . . how much, Scott?"

I considered the question. It was a good one—and, of course, it was one I'd asked myself on more than one of those sleepless nights. "Quite a lot," I said. "Also, quite a lot of relief, I won't lie about that. If Mr. Yow, Git Down was a real person, he'd never have to pick up another restaurant tab. Not when I was with him, at least." I paused. "Does that shock you?"

She reached across the table and briefly touched my hand. "Not even a little."

Hearing her say that made me feel better than I would have believed. I gave her hand a brief squeeze and then let it go. "What's your other question?"

"How important to you is it that I believe your story about these things coming back?"

I thought this was an excellent question, even though the Lucite cube was right there next to the sugar bowl. Such items are not exactly rare, after all. And I thought that if she *had* majored in psychology rather than German, she probably would have done fine.

"Not as important as I thought an hour ago," I said. "Just telling it has been a help."

She nodded and smiled. "Good. Now here's my best guess: someone is very likely playing a game with you. Not a nice one."

"Trickin' on me," I said. I tried not to show it, but I'd rarely been so disappointed. Maybe a layer of disbelief settles over people in certain circumstances, protecting them. Or maybe—probably—I hadn't conveyed my own sense that this thing was just . . . happening. *Still* happening. The way avalanches do.

"Trickin' on you," she agreed, and then: "But you don't believe it."

More points for perception. I nodded. "I locked the door when I went out, and it was locked when I came back from Staples. I heard the clunk the tumblers make when they turn. They're loud. You can't miss them."

"Still . . . survivor guilt is a funny thing. And powerful, at least according to the magazines."

"This . . ." *This isn't survivor guilt* was what I meant to say, but it would have been the wrong thing. I had a fighting chance to make a new friend here, and having a new friend would be good, no matter how the rest of this came out. So I amended it. "I don't think this is survivor guilt." I pointed to the Lucite cube. "It's right there, isn't it? Like Sonja's sunglasses. You see it. I do, too. I suppose I could have bought it myself, but . . ." I shrugged, trying to convey what we both surely knew: *anything* is possible.

"I don't think you did that. But neither can I accept the idea that a trapdoor opened between reality and the Twilight Zone and these things fell out."

Yes, that was the problem. For Paula the idea that the Lucite cube and the other things which had appeared in my apartment had some supernatural origin was automatically off-limits, no matter how much the facts might seem to support the idea. What I needed to do was to decide if I needed to argue the point more than I needed to make a friend.

I decided I did not.

"All right," I said. I caught the waiter's eye and made a check-writing gesture in the air. "I can accept your inability to accept."

"Can you?" she asked, looking at me closely.

"Yes." And I thought it was true. "If, that is, we could have a cup of coffee from time to time. Or just say hi in the lobby."

"Absolutely." But she sounded absent, not really in the conversation. She was looking at the Lucite cube with the steel penny inside it. Then she looked up at me. I could almost see a lightbulb appearing over her head, like in a cartoon. She reached out and grasped the cube with one hand. I could never convey the depth of the dread I felt when she did that, but what could I say? We were New Yorkers in a clean, well-lighted place. For her part, she'd already laid down the ground rules, and they pretty firmly excluded the supernatural. The supernatural was out of bounds. Anything hit there was a do-over.

And there was a light in Paula's eyes. One that suggested Ms.

Yow, Git Down was in the house, and I know from personal experience that's a hard voice to resist.

"Give it to me," she proposed, smiling into my eyes. When she did that I could see—for the first time, really—that she was sexy as well as pretty.

"Why?" As if I didn't know.

"Call it my fee for listening to your story."

"I don't know if that's such a good—"

"It is, though," she said. She was warming to her own inspiration, and when people do that, they rarely take no for an answer. "It's a *great* idea. I'll make sure this piece of memorabilia at least doesn't come back to you, wagging its tail behind it. We've got a safe in the apartment." She made a charming little pantomime gesture of shutting a safe door, twirling the combination, and then throwing the key back over her shoulder.

"All right," I said. "It's my gift to you." And I felt something that might have been mean-spirited gladness. Call it the voice of Mr. Yow, You'll Find Out. Apparently just getting it off my chest wasn't enough, after all. She hadn't believed me, and at least part of me *did* want to be believed and resented Paula for not getting what it wanted. That part knew that letting her take the Lucite cube was an absolutely terrible idea, but was glad to see her tuck it away in her purse, just the same.

"There," she said briskly. "Mama say bye-bye, make all gone. Maybe when it doesn't come back in a week—or two, I guess it all depends on how stubborn your subconscious wants to be—you can start giving the rest of the things away." And her saying that was her real gift to me that day, although I didn't know it then.

"Maybe so," I said, and smiled. Big smile for the new friend. Big smile for pretty Mama. All the time thinking, You'll find out.

Yow.

She did.

Three nights later, while I was watching Chuck Scarborough explain the city's latest transit woes on the six o'clock news, my doorbell rang. Since no one had been announced, I assumed it was a package, maybe even Rafe with something from Federal Express. I opened the door and there stood Paula Robeson.

This was not the woman with whom I'd had lunch. Call this version of Paula Ms. Yow, Ain't That Chemotherapy *Nasty*. She was wearing a little lipstick but nothing else in the way of makeup, and her complexion was a sickly shade of yellow-white. There were dark brownish-purple arcs under her eyes. She might have given her hair a token swipe with the brush before coming down from the fifth floor, but it hadn't done much good. It looked like straw and stuck out on either side of her head in a way that would have been comic-strip funny under other circumstances. She was holding the Lucite cube up in front of her breasts, allowing me to note that the well-kept nails on that hand were gone. She'd chewed them away, right down to the quick. And my first thought, God help me, was *yep, she found out*.

She held it out to me. "Take it back," she said.

I did so without a word.

"His name was Roland Abelson," she said. "Wasn't it?"

"Yes."

"He had red hair."

"Yes."

"Not married but paying child support to a woman in Rahway."

I hadn't known that—didn't believe *anyone* at Light and Bell had known that—but I nodded again, and not just to keep her rolling. I was sure she was right. "What was her name, Paula?" Not knowing why I was asking, not yet, just knowing I had to know.

"Tonya Gregson." It was as if she was in a trance. There was something in her eyes, though, something so terrible I could hardly stand to look at it. Nevertheless, I stored the name away. *Tonya Gregson, Rahway*. And then, like some guy doing stockroom inventory: *One Lucite cube with penny inside*.

"He tried to crawl under his desk, did you know that? No, I can see you didn't. His hair was on fire and he was crying. Because in that instant he understood he was never going to own a catamaran or even mow his lawn again." She reached out and put a hand on my cheek, a gesture so intimate it would have been shocking had her hand not been so cold. "At the end, he would have given every cent he had, and every stock option he held, just to be able to mow his lawn again. Do you believe that?"

"Yes."

"The place was full of screams, he could smell jet fuel, and *he un-*

derstood it was his dying hour. Do you understand that? Do you understand the *enormity* of that?"

I nodded. I couldn't speak. You could have put a gun to my head
and I still wouldn't have been able to speak.

"The politicians talk about memorials and courage and wars to
end terrorism, but burning hair is apolitical." She bared her teeth in
an unspeakable grin. A moment later it was gone. "He was trying to
crawl under his desk with his hair on fire. There was a plastic thing
under his desk, a what-do-you-call it—"

"Mat—"

"Yes, a mat, a plastic mat, and his hands were on that and he
could feel the ridges in the plastic and smell his own burning hair.
Do you understand that?"

I nodded. I started to cry. It was Roland Abelson we were talking
about, this guy I used to work with. He was in Liability and I didn't
know him very well. To say hi to is all; how was I supposed to know
he had a kid in Rahway? And if I hadn't played hooky that day, my
hair probably would have burned, too. I'd never really understood
that before.

"I don't want to see you again," she said. She flashed her grue-
some grin once more, but now she was crying, too. "I don't care
about your problems. I don't care about any of the shit you found.
We're quits. From now on you leave me alone." She started to turn
away, then turned back. She said: "They did it in the name of God,
but there is no God. If there was a God, Mr. Staley, He would have
struck all eighteen of them dead in their boarding lounges with their
boarding passes in their hands, but no God did. They called for passengers to get on and those fucks just got on."

I watched her walk back to the elevator. Her back was very stiff.
Her hair stuck out on either side of her head, making her look like a
girl in a Sunday Funnies cartoon. She didn't want to see me anymore,
and I didn't blame her. I closed the door and looked at the steel Abe
Lincoln in the Lucite cube. I looked at him for quite a long time. I
thought about how the hair of his beard would have smelled if U.S.
Grant had stuck one of his everlasting cigars in it. That unpleasant
frying aroma. On TV, someone was saying that there was a mattress
blowout going on at Sleepy's. After that, Len Berman came on and
talked about the Jets.

That night I woke up at two in the morning, listening to the voices whisper. I hadn't had any dreams or visions of the people who owned the objects, hadn't seen anyone with their hair on fire or jumping from the windows to escape the burning jet fuel, but why would I? I knew who they were, and the things they left behind had been left for me. Letting Paula Robeson take the Lucite cube had been wrong, but only because she was the wrong person.

And speaking of Paula, one of the voices was hers. *You can start giving the rest of the things away,* it said. And it said, *I guess it all depends on how stubborn your subconscious wants to be.*

I lay back down and after a while I was able to go to sleep. I dreamed I was in Central Park, feeding the ducks, when all at once there was a loud noise like a sonic boom and smoke filled the sky. In my dream, the smoke smelled like burning hair.

I thought about Tonya Gregson in Rahway—Tonya and the child who might or might not have Roland Abelson's eyes—and thought I'd have to work up to that one. I decided to start with Bruce Mason's widow.

I took the train to Dobbs Ferry and called a taxi from the station. The cabbie took me to a Cape Cod house on a residential street. I gave him some money, told him to wait—I wouldn't be long—and rang the doorbell. I had a box under one arm. It looked like the kind that contains a bakery cake.

I only had to ring once, because I'd called ahead and Janice Mason was expecting me. I had my story carefully prepared and told it with some confidence, knowing that the taxi sitting in the driveway, its meter running, would forestall any detailed cross-examination.

On September seventh, I said—the Friday before—I had tried to blow a note from the conch Bruce kept on his desk, as I had heard Bruce himself do at the Jones Beach picnic. (Janice, Mrs. Lord of the Flies, nodding; she had been there, of course.) Well, I said, to make a long story short, I had persuaded Bruce to let me have the conch shell over the weekend so I could practice. Then, on Monday morning, I'd awakened with a raging sinus infection and a horrible headache to go with it. (This was a story I had already told several people.) I'd been drinking a cup of tea when I heard the boom and saw the rising smoke. I hadn't thought of the conch shell again until just this week. I'd been cleaning out my little utility closet and by damn, there it was. And I just thought . . . well, it's not much of a keepsake, but I just thought maybe you'd like to . . . you know . . .

Her eyes filled up with tears just as mine had when Paula brought back Roland Abelson's "retirement fund," only these weren't accompanied by the look of fright that I'm sure was on my own face as Paula stood there with her stiff hair sticking out on either side of her head. Janice told me she would be glad to have any keepsake of Bruce.

"I can't get over the way we said good-bye," she said, holding the box in her arms. "He always left very early because he took the train. He kissed me on the cheek and I opened one eye and asked him if he'd bring back a pint of Half and Half. He said he would. That's the last thing he ever said to me. When he asked me to marry him, I felt like Helen of Troy—stupid but absolutely true—and I wish I'd said something better than 'Bring home a pint of Half and Half.' But we'd been married a long time, and it seemed like business as usual that day, and . . . we don't know, do we?"

"No."

"Yes. Any parting could be forever, and we don't know. Thank you, Mr. Staley. For coming out and bringing me this. That was very kind." She smiled a little then. "Do you remember how he stood on the beach with his shirt off and blew it?"

"Yes," I said, and looked at the way she held the box. Later she would sit down and take the shell out and hold it on her lap and cry. I knew that the conch, at least, would never come back to my apartment. It was home.

I returned to the station and caught the train back to New York. The cars were almost empty at that time of day, early afternoon, and I sat by a rain- and dirt-streaked window, looking out at the river and the approaching skyline. On cloudy and rainy days, you almost seem to be creating that skyline out of your own imagination, a piece at a time.

Tomorrow I'd go to Rahway, with the penny in the Lucite cube. Perhaps the child would take it in his or her chubby hand and look at it curiously. In any case, it would be out of my life. I thought the only difficult thing to get rid of would be Jimmy Eagleton's Farting Cushion—I could hardly tell Mrs. Eagleton I'd brought it home for the weekend in order to practice using it, could I? But necessity is the mother of invention, and I was confident that I would eventually think of some halfway plausible story.

It occurred to me that other things might show up, in time. And I'd be lying if I told you I found that possibility entirely unpleasant. When it comes to returning things which people believe have been lost forever, things that have *weight*, there are compensations. Even if they're only little things, like a pair of joke sunglasses or a steel penny in a Lucite cube . . . yeah. I'd have to say there are compensations.

WALTER MOSLEY

Walter Mosley has forged a successful mystery career in the tradition of authors like Chester Himes and Carroll John Daly, but he added the complex issue of race relations and an in-depth look at the lethal heart of a major city that few authors can even come close to. He is the author of twenty books and has been translated into twenty-one languages. His popular mysteries featuring Easy Rawlins and his friend Raymond "Mouse" Alexander began with *Devil in a Blue Dress*, which was made into the film of the same name starring Denzel Washington and Jennifer Beals. Others in the series were *A Red Death*, *White Butterfly*, *Black Betty*, *A Little Yellow Dog*, and *Bad Boy Brawly Brown*; a prequel to the Rawlins mysteries, *Gone Fishin'*, and a series of short stories collected in *Six Easy Pieces*. His other character, ex-con Socrates Fortlow, lives in Los Angeles, infusing his episodic tales with ethical and political considerations. Excerpts from his collection *Always Outnumbered, Always Outgunned: The Socrates Fortlow Stories* have been published in *Esquire*, *GQ*, *USA Weekend*, *Buzz*, and *Mary Higgins Clark Mystery Magazine*. One of these new stories was an O. Henry Award winner for 1996 and is featured in *Prize Stories 1996: The O. Henry Awards*, edited by William Abraham. In 1996 he was named the first Artist-in-Residence at the Africana Studies Institute, New York University. Since that residency, he has continued to work with the department, creating an innovative lecture series entitled "Black Genius" which brings diverse speakers from art, politics, and academe to discuss practical solutions to contemporary issues. Designed as a "public classroom" these lectures have included speakers ranging from Spike Lee to Angela Davis. In February 1999, a collection of these lectures was published with the title *Black Genius*, with a Mosley introduction and essay. This past year, Mosley returned to the mystery world with the debut of a new series. *Fearless Jones* is now available. Set in 1950s Los Angeles and introducing secondhand bookstore owner Paris Minton and his best friend, war veteran Fearless Jones, the novel is already garnering early praise. His most recent novels include a look at men in shades of black and white, in *The Man in My Basement*, the novel *47* and, featuring Easy Rawlins, *Little Scarlet* and *Cinnamon Kiss*.

ARCHIBALD LAWLESS, ANARCHIST AT LARGE:
WALKING THE LINE

Walter Mosley

1

I saw the first ad on a Tuesday in the *Wall Street Journal*.

> REQUIRED: SCRIBE
> A. LAWLESS IN THE TESSLA BUILDING

The next notice appeared on Thursday in the classified section of the daily *New York Times*.

> AAL LTD. SEEKS SCRIBE
> APPLY AT OFFICES IN TESSLA BUILDING

Then, the next week, on the back page of the *Village Voice* and in the classified section of the *Amsterdam News*.

> SCRIBE SOUGHT KL-5-8713

The last ads gave no address but I knew that it had to be put there by A. Lawless at AAL Ltd. in the Tessla Building. I called and got an answering machine.

"If you are applying for the position leave your name and number," a throaty woman's voice said. "And please let us know where you heard about the position."

Then came the tone.

"Felix Orlean," I said. I gave my phone number and added, "I saw your ad in the *Times*, the *Journal*, the *Amsterdan News*, and the *Village Voice*."

Much later that night, hours after I'd gone to sleep, the phone rang giving me a sudden fright. I was sure that my mother or father had gotten sick down home. I grabbed the phone and whined, "What? What's wrong?"

"Mr. Orlean?" He said *or-leen* not *or-le-ahn* as I pronounce my name.

"Yes? What's wrong?"

"Nothing's wrong, son," he sad in a deep gravelly voice that reminded me of Wallace Beery from the old films. "Why would you think something's wrong?"

"What time is it?"

"I just went through the tape," he said. "You were the only one who saw all four ads. Do you read all those New York papers?"

"Yeah," I said. "The *Washington Post* too. And the *International Herald Tribune* when I can get it."

I turned on the light next to my bed to see the clock but was blinded by the glare.

"Are you a student?" he asked.

"Yeah," I said. "At Columbia." If I had been more awake I wouldn't have been so open.

"Come to the office this morning," he said. "I'll be in by five but you don't have to get there till ten to six."

"Huh?"

He hung up and my eyesight cleared enough to see that it was three forty-five.

I wondered what kind of man did his work at that time. And what would possess him to call a potential employee hours before the sun came up? Was he crazy? Must be, I thought. Of course I had no intention of going to his office at six A.M. or at any other time. I turned out the light and pulled the covers up to my chin but sleep did not return.

I had been intrigued for days about the job description of *scribe*. I had thought it was just a fancy way to say secretary who takes dicta-tion. But after the call I wasn't so sure. Who was A. Lawless? Was it that cool woman's voice on the answering machine? No. It had to be the raspy late-night caller.

What kind of job could it be?

"It's too bad yo' daddy and them named you Felix," Aunt Al-berta, the Ninth Ward fence, said to me once. And when I asked her why she said, " 'Cause that's a cartoon cat and we all know what cu-riosity do for a cat."

I loved my Aunt Alberta. She's the one who encouraged me when I wanted to come up to New York to study journalism. My parents had always planned on me becoming a lawyer like my fa-ther, and his father. Even my great grandfather had studied law, al-though he wasn't able to get a license to practice in Louisiana. In those days colored lawyers, even extremely light ones, were rare down south.

My father had harangued me for a week to stop my foolishness and make a decision about which law school to attend. I finally told him that Alberta thought it was a good idea for me to try journalism.

"And how would you know what Alberta thinks?" he asked. My father is a big man but I'm just small, taking after the men on my mother's side.

"I asked her," I said shaking a little under the shadow of JP Orlean.

"You what?"

"I went down to the county jail and saw her, poppa." I closed my eyes involuntarily, expecting to be knocked on my can.

I had been hit by my father before. He was a violent man. *Stern but fair*, my mother used to say. But I never saw what was fair about whipping a child with a strap until red welts rose up all over his body.

"I thought I told you that Alberta Hadity is no longer to be con-sidered family," my father said in a voice as quiet as the breeze.

And that was my chance. After twenty-one years of obeying my father, or lying to him, the gate was open. All I had to do was stay quiet. All I had to do was keep my mouth shut and he would see it as insubordination.

I looked down at his brown shoes. Blutcher's we called them down south. They're known as wing tips in New York. Chub Wilkie, I knew, had shined those shoes that morning. He shined my father's shoes every week day morning. JP used to say that Chub Wilkie was the finest man in the law building where he practiced. But he never invited Mr. Wilkie to dinner as he did the law partners at Hermann, Bledsoe, and Orlean.

Mr. Wilkie was too dark-skinned and too poor to be seen on our social level.

My father and mother were no more than café au lait in their coloring. My sister and I were lighter even than that.

"Well?" my father said. I could feel the weight of his stare on my neck.

It was a great concession for him to ask anything of me. I was supposed to say that I was sorry, that I would never speak to my felon auntie again. The words formed in my mouth but I kept my teeth clamped down on them.

"I expect you out of the house before your mother returns home," he said.

But still he hesitated.

I knew that he expected me to fold, to gasp out an apology and beg for his indulgence. I had always lived at home, never worked a day in my life. But as dependent as I was on my father I was just as stubborn too.

After another minute the shoes carried him from the family den. I looked up and out of the glass doors that led to the garden at the back of the house. I knew then that it would be the last time I ever saw my mother's orchid and lily garden.

I almost yelled for joy.

After reliving my exile from the Orlean family sleep was impossible. At five I got out of bed and went to the tiny kitchen that separated my room from my soccer-star roommate, Lonnie McKay. I heated water in a saucepan instead of the kettle so as not to wake him.

Lonnie had a full scholarship in the engineering school for captaining the fledgling Columbia Ciceros (pronounced by those in the know as Kickeros). I had to borrow the thirty thousand dollars a year and then get part-time jobs to pay the outrageous rent and for anything else I might need—like instant coffee.

I poured the hot water and mixed in the freeze-dried flakes. The coffee was bitter and yet tasteless but that was all right by me. The bitter taste was my life, that's what I was thinking.

And then I looked up.

The long red velvet curtain that covered Lonnie's doorway fluttered and a young woman walked through. There was only the small forty-watt bulb lighting the kitchen but I could see that she was naked except for the tan bikini panties. An inch shorter than I with smallish but shapely breasts. Her hair was long curly brown and her eyes were large. She was slender and pale skinned but somehow I knew that she was a colored woman, girl really—not more than nineteen. When she saw me she smiled, crossed her hands over her breasts, and sat down on the chair across from where I was standing.

"Hi," she said, smiling with false modesty.

"Hi." I looked away to hide my embarrassment.

"You must be Felix."

Forcing my head back I looked her in the eye. Eyes. They were light brown and laughing, full of life and encouraging me to stay where I was, not to run back to my room which is what I wanted to do more than anything.

"Yes," I said. I stepped forward and held out my hand like I always did when someone called me by name.

She looked at my hand, hesitated, then shifted, managing to keep her modesty and take my hand at the same time.

"Arrett," she said. "I'm a friend of Lonnie's."

"Pleased to meet you," I said.

We stared at each other for a moment, and then a moment more. Arrett seemed to be suppressing a laugh. I would have loved to see that laugh.

"Why are you up so early?" she asked.

"Going to apply for a job," I said. And there it was. My future was sealed. A near naked woman stumbling across my path in the early hours of the morning and I was thrown out of my orbit. My whole life had changed because of a girl I'd probably never see again.

Mr. Lawless would have said that it was my fate, that the moment he heard my light New Orleans drawl he knew that we were meant to come together.

"What kind of job?" she asked.

"I don't know."

She grinned and I felt my heart swell up in my chest.

A sound issued from Lonnie's room. It might have been her name.

"He wants me," she said. It was almost a question.

I almost said, *don't go*.

"Ari," Lonnie called from behind the red curtain.

She got up, forgetting her modesty, and said, "We'll see each other at school," and then ran through the red fabric into my roommate's den.

I sat down and considered going back to bed. But then Lonnie's first sigh of pleasure pierced the air. I hurried to my room, dressed and left the apartment before they could fill the house with their love.

2

The Tessla building is on West 38th Street. It's not the biggest building in midtown Manhattan but it's up there. Sixty-nine stories. The glass doors are modern but the lobby is thirties art deco to the max. Black, white, and red tiles of marble cover the floor in vaguely Egyptian designs. The marble on the walls is gray and light blue. A huge painting behind the guard's stone counter is of a bare-breasted, golden skinned Joan of Arc leading her French army out of a sun that you just know represents God.

"Yes?" the guard asked me. "Can I help you?"

"AAL Limited," I said.

The man behind the counter was African, I believed. His features were purely Negroid. The round head and almost almond shaped eyes, the dark skin had no blemishes and his lips seemed chiseled they were so perfect. My sister went out with a man like this for two weeks once and our parents decided to send her to Paris for two years. She was still there for all that I knew.

The man's eyes rose as a smile curved his sensual mouth.

"Mr. Lawless wants to see you?"

"I guess," I said. "He said to get here by ten to six."

"That's Mr. Lawless. No visitors after five fifty-five. He told me that himself," the guard said, sounding a little like he'd learned to speak English from an Englishman. "What do you do?"

"I'm a student," I said. "I study journalism."

This answer seemed to disappoint the young guard. He shrugged his shoulders as if to say, too bad.

"Fifty-two eleven," he said. "Take the last elevator on the right. It's the only one we have working this early."

It was a utility elevator. Thick matting like gray bedspreads were hung over the walls to protect them from harm when heavy objects were moved. I pushed the button and the door closed but there was no sense of motion. A couple of times I looked up at the small screen that should have shown the floors as they passed by but the number was stuck at twelve.

Finally, after a long interval the doors opened and I got out wondering if I was on the right floor. The walls were painted the palest possible green and the floor was tiled with white stone veined in violet and dark jade. Two arrows on the wall opposite the elevator door pointed in either direction. Right was 5220 to 5244 and left was 5200 to 5219.

I turned left. After I passed the first few offices I realized that the door at the dead end of the hall was my destination.

That door was different than the rest. From the distance it seemed to be boarded up as if it were under construction or condemned. Five or six weathered boards were nailed into place, lengthwise but not neatly at all. Two shorter boards were nailed across these, more or less vertically. There was something that I couldn't discern hanging midway down the left side of the door.

I passed Tweed's Beads and then Thunderstruck, Personal Dating Service. I was wondering what other kind of date there was, other than personal that is, when I realized that the object hanging from the door at the end of the hall was a handmade doll with a black face and a striped yellow and red dress. The dress was painted on the cylindrical body made from a toilet paper roll or something like that.

The voodoo doll stopped me for moment. I'd seen many such fetishes in Louisiana. They're all over the French Quarter, for tourists mainly. But hanging there, from that boarded-up door, the manißkin took on a sinister air.

What the hell was a voodoo doll doing there on the fifty-second floor of a skyscraper in New York City?

I gritted my teeth and took a deep breath through my nostrils. Then I walked forward.

There wasn't any doorknob or door that I could see. Just the

grayed planking nailed to either side of the doorway covering something black and wooden behind. The doll had a slack grin painted on
her round head. She seemed to be leering at me.

"Go on," I said to the doll.

I rapped on the boards.

No answer.

After a reasonable pause I knocked again.

No answer.

My fear of the doll was quickly being replaced by fury. What
kind of trick was being played on me? Was the guard downstairs in
on it? Did Lonnie put Arrett out there to run me out of the house?

My fingernails were pressing hard against my palms when a voice
said, "Who's out there?"

There was no mistaking that raspy tone.

"Mr. Lawless?"

"Orleen?"

"Yes. I mean yes sir." The latter was added because I was raised
on good manners down home.

The door opened into the room, which surprised me. The planks
were arranged to give the illusion of a boarded-up portal but really
they were cut to allow the door, boards and all, to open inward.

The man standing there before me had no double in the present
day world or in history. He stood a solid six three or four with skin
that was deep amber. His hair, which was mostly dark brown and
gray, had some reddish highlights twined into a forest of thick dread-
locks that went straight out nine inches from his head, sagging only
slightly. The hair resembled a royal headdress, maybe even a crown
of thorns but Mr. A. Lawless was no victim. His chest and shoulders
were unusually broad even for a man his size. His eyes were small
and deep set. The forehead was round and his high cheekbones cut
strong slanting lines down to his chin which gave his face a definite
heart shape. There was no facial hair and no wrinkles except at the
corners of his eyes.

His stomach protruded from his open fatigue jacket but it didn't
sag or seem soft against the buttoned-up rose colored shirt. His pants
were tan and shapeless. His big feet were bare.

A. Lawless was forty-five or maybe sixty. But even a rowdy with a
baseball bat would have thought twice before taking a swing at him.

"Orleen?" he asked me again.

"Yes sir."

"Come in, come." He gestured with hands that were small compared to the rest of the him. But that only reminded me of stories I'd read about the Brown Bomber, Joe Louis. He had small hands too.

Mr. Lawless went around me to close the boarded door. He threw three bolts down the side and then flipped down a bronze piece of metal at the base that served a buttress against anyone forcing their way in.

"Just so we don't have any unwanted guests," he said. Then he led the way back to the interior.

I followed my host through a moderate sized room that had a dark wood floor and wooden furniture that wasn't of this century or the last. Just a couple of tables with a chair and a cushionless couch. The thick pieces had seen a lot of use in the past hundred years or so but they were well varnished and sturdy.

There were two doors at the back of the room. Straight ahead was a frosted glass door that had no writing on it. Immediately to the left was an oak door upon which the word STORAGE was stenciled in highlighted gold lettering.

We went through the untitled glass door into a smallish room that I figured to be his office. At the back of the room was a window that had an unobstructed view of the Hudson River and New Jersey beyond. It was about six and the sun was just falling upon our misty neighbor state. There was a dark wood swivel chair next to the window, behind a small desk which was only large enough for the laptop computer that sat on it.

The room was filled with a musky odor that, while neither sweet nor sour, carried a pleasant notion. This odor I later came to associate with Archibald Lawless's life. He pervaded any situation with his presence and half-civilized genius.

The wall to my left had a series of shelves that held various oddities. There was a crusty old toy chest and a child's baby doll with a red sash around its throat. There was a rattlesnake suspended in fluid in a large jar, a parchment scroll tied with string, a replica of a human skull, a small stuffed animal (I didn't know what species at the time), and a necklace: a piece of costume jewelry in a plastic case held up by a W-shaped metal frame. This necklace was made up of gaudy pieces of glass representing emeralds and rubies mainly, with a ribbon of fake diamonds snaking through. There were other pieces on the shelves but that's all I was able to make out on first sight.

The wall opposite the shelves was dominated by a giant blown-up photograph rendered in sepia tones. It was the face of some German or Russian from a bygone age. The man, whoever he was, had a big mustache and a wild look in his eye. I would have said it was a picture of Nietzsche but I knew it wasn't him because I had just finished reading *Thus Spoke Zarathustra* for a class called the History of the West and there was a photograph of the German philosopher on the cover of the book.

"Bakunin," A. Lawless said. "It's Bakunin."

"The anarchist?"

"He's why I'm here today talking to you. And he's why you're here today talking to me."

"Oh," I said trying to think of a way into the conversation.

"Sit down," the big man said.

I noticed that there were two tree trunks diagonally across from the swivel chair. Real tree trunks, plucked right out of the ground. Each one was about two and a half feet high with curves carved into them for a comfortable seat.

I sat.

"Archibald Lawless Anarchist at Large," my host said formally. He sat in the swivel chair and leaned back.

"What does that mean exactly?"

"What do you think it means?"

"That you plan to overthrow the government in hopes of causing a perpetual state of chaos throughout the world?"

"They aren't much on reality at Xavier or Columbia, are they?"

I didn't remember telling him that I did my undergrad work at Xavier but I didn't remember much before Arrett.

"What do you do?" I asked.

"I walk the line."

"What line?"

"Not," he said raising an instructive finger, "what line but the line between what forces?"

"Okay," I said. "The line between what forces?"

"I walk the line between chaos and the man."

3

Archibald Lawless brought two fingers to his lower lip speculating, it seemed, about me and how I would fill the job opening.

But by then I had decided against taking the position. I found his presence disturbing. If he offered me a cup of tea I'd take it out of civility, but I wouldn't swallow a drop.

Still, I was intrigued. The line between chaos and the man seemed a perfect personal realization of the philosophy he followed. It brought to mind a wild creature out at the edges of some great, decaying civilization. Interesting for a college paper but not as a profession.

I had just begun considering how to refuse if he offered me the job when a knock came on the front door of the office. Three fast raps and then two slower ones.

"Get that will you, Felix?" Lawless said.

I didn't want to sound off so I went back through the Americana room and said, "Yes," through the door.

"Carlos for A L," a slightly Spanish, slightly street accented voice answered.

I didn't know what to do so I threw the locks, kicked up the buttress, and opened the door.

The man was my height, slight and obviously with a preoccupation for the color green. He wore a forest green three-button suit over a pale green shirt with a skinny dark green tie.

His shoes were reptile definitely and also green. His skin was olive. He was past forty, maybe past fifty.

"Hey, bro," Carlos said and I really didn't know what to make of him.

"Wait here please," I said.

He nodded and I went back to Archibald Lawless's office. The anarchist was sitting back in his chair, waiting for my report.

"It's a guy named Carlos. He's all in green. I didn't ask what he wanted."

"Come on in, Carlos!" Archibald shouted.

The green man came in pushing open the office door.

"Hey, Mr. Big," Carlos greeted.

"What you got for me?"

"Not too much. They say he was drinking, she wasn't but she was just some girl he'd picked up at the bar."

"Couldn't you get any more?" Lawless wasn't upset but there was a certain insistence to his query.

"Maria tried, man, but they don't have it on the computer and the written files were sent to Arizona three hours after they were done. The only reason she got that much was that she knows a guy who works in filing. He sneaked a look for her."

Lawless turned away from Carlos and me and looked out over New Jersey.

"How's your mother?" Lawless asked Hoboken.

"She's fine," Carlos responded. "And Petey's doin' real good in that school you got him into."

"Tell him hello for me when you see him," Lawless said. He swiveled around and leveled his murky eyes at the green man. "See you later, Carlos."

"You got it, Mr. Big. Any time."

Carlos turned to go. I noticed that he seemed nervous. Not necessarily scared but definitely happy to be going. I followed him to the front door and threw all the locks into place after him.

When I returned Lawless was pulling on heavy work boots. He nodded toward a tree stump and I sat.

"Do you know what a scribe does?" he asked.

"I don't know if I'm really interested—"

"Do you know what a scribe does?" he asked again, cutting me off.

"They were monks or something," I said. "They wrote out copies of the bible before there was printing or moveable type."

"That's correct," he said sounding like one of my professors. "They also wrote for illiterate lords. Contracts, peace treaties, even love letters." Lawless smiled. "How much do you know about Bakunin?"

"Just his name."

"He was a great man. He knew about all the gross injustices of Stalin before Stalin was born. He was probably the greatest political thinker of the twentieth century and he didn't even live in that century. But do you know what was wrong with him?"

"No sir."

"He was a man of action and so he didn't spend enough time writing cohesive documents of his ideas. Don't get me wrong, he wrote a lot. But he never created a comprehensive document detailing a clear idea of anarchist political organization. After he died the writing he left behind made many small-minded men see him as a crackpot and a fool. I don't intend for my legacy to be treated like that."

"And that's why you need a scribe?"

"Mainly." He turned to watch Jersey again. "But also I need a simple transcriber. Someone to take my notes and scribbles and to make sense out of them. To document what I'm trying to do."

"That's all?"

"Mostly. There'll be some errands. Maybe even a little research, you know—investigative work. But any good journalism student should love doing some field work."

"I didn't tell you I was a journalism student."

"No, you didn't. But I know a lot about you, Felix Orlean," he said, pronouncing my name correctly this time. "That's why I put that old doll of mine on the door, I wanted to see if you were superstitious. I know about your father too, Justin Proudfoot Orlean, a big time lawyer down in Louisiana. And your mother, Katherine Hadity, was a medical student before she married your father and decided to commit her life to you and your sister Rachel who now goes by the name Angela in the part of London called Brixton."

He might as well have hit me over the head with a twelve-pound ham. I didn't know that my mother had been a medical student but it made sense since she had always wanted Rachel to be a doctor. I didn't know that Rachel had moved to England.

"Where'd you get all that?"

"And that's another thing." Lawless cut his eyes at the laptop on the tiny desk. Then he held up that educational finger. "No work that you do for me goes on the computer. I want to wait until we get it right to let the world in on our work."

"I'm not w-working for you, Mr. Lawless," I said, hating myself for the stutter skip.

"Why not?"

"I don't know what you do for one thing," I said. "And I don't like people calling me at any hour of the night. You have your doors boarded up and you call yourself an anarchist. Some guy who looks like a street thug comes in to make some kind of report."

"I told you what I do. I'm an anarchist who wants to keep everything straight. From the crazed politico who decides that he can interfere with the rights of others because he's got some inside track on the truth to the fascist mayor trying to shut down the little guy so he can fill his coffers with gold while reinventing the police state.

"I'm the last honest man, an eastern cowboy. And you, Mr. Orlean, you are a young man trying to make something of himself. Your father's a rich man but you pay your own way. He wanted you to become a lawyer, I bet, and you turned your back on him in order to be your own man. That's half the way to me, Felix. Why not see what more there is?"

"I can take care of my own life, Mr. Lawless," I said. "The only thing I need from a job is money."

"How much money?"

"Well, my rent which is five-fifty a month and then my other expenses. . . ."

"So you need forty-two thousand, before taxes, that is if you pay taxes." I had come up with the same number after an afternoon of budgeting.

"Of course I pay my taxes," I said.

"Of course you do," Lawless said, smiling broadly. "I'll pay you what you need for this position. All you have to do is agree to try it out for a few weeks."

I glanced at the blow-up of Bakunin and thought about the chance this might be. I needed the money. My parents wouldn't even answer one of my letters much less finance my education.

"I'm not sure," I said.

"About what?"

"The line you're talking about," I said. "It sounds like some kind of legal boundary. One side is law abiding and the other isn't."

"You're just an employee, Felix. Like anyone working for Enron or Hasbro. No one there is held responsible for what their employers may or may not have done."

"I won't do anything illegal."

"Of course you won't," Lawless said.

"I have to put my school work first."

"We can make your hours flexible."

"If I don't like what's happening I'll quit immediately," I said. "No prior notice."

"You sound more like a law student than a news hound," Lawless said. "But believe me I need you, Felix. I don't have the time to read every paper. If I know you're going through five or six of the big ones that'll take a lot of pressure off of me. And you'll learn a lot here. I've been around. From the guest of royalty in Asia to the prisons of Turkey and Mexico."

"No law breaking for me," I said again.

"I heard you." Lawless took a piece of paper from the ledge on the window behind him and handed it to me. "Over the next couple of days I'd like you to check up on these people."

"What do you mean?"

"Nothing questionable, simply check to see that they're around. Try to talk to them yourself but if you can't just make sure that they're there, and that they're okay."

"You think these people might be in trouble?"

"I don't worry about dolls hanging from doorknobs," he said. "They don't mean a thing to me. I'm just looking into a little problem that I picked up on the other day."

"Maybe you should call the police."

"The police and I have a deal. I don't talk to them and they don't listen to me. It works out just fine."

4

I wanted to talk more but Lawless said that he had his day cut out for him.

"I've got to go out but you can stay," he said. "The room next door will be your workplace. Here let me show you."

My new employer stood up. As I said, he's a big man. There seemed to be something important in even this simple movement. It was as if some stone monolith were suddenly sentient and moving with singular purpose in the world.

The room labeled STORAGE was narrow, crowded with boxes and untidy. There was a long table covered with papers, both printed and handwritten, and various publications. The boxes were cardboard, some white and some brown. The white ones had handwritten single letters on their fitted lids, scrawled in red. The brown ones on the whole were open at the top with all sorts of files and papers stacked inside.

"The white ones are my filing cabinet," Lawless said. "The

brown ones are waiting for you to put them in order. There's a flat stack of unconstructed file boxes in the corner under the window. When you need a new one just put it together." He waved at a pile of rags set upon something in the corner.

"What's that?" I asked, pointing at a pink metal box that sat directly under the window.

"It's the only real file cabinet but we don't keep files in there." He didn't say anything else about it and I was too busy trying to keep up to care.

Through the window an ocean liner was making its way up river. It was larger than three city blocks.

"The papers are all different," Lawless said. "The legal sheets are my journal entries, reports, and notes. These you are to transcribe. The mimeod sheets are various documents that have come to me. I need you to file them according to the way the rest of the files work. If you have any questions just ask me."

The liner let out a blast from its horn that I heard faintly through the closed window.

"And these newsletters," he said and then paused.

"What about them?"

"These newsletters I get from different places. They're very, very specialized." He was holding up a thick stack of printed materials. "Some of them come from friends around the world. Anarchist and syndicalist communes in America and elsewhere, in the country and the cities too. One of them's an Internet commune. That one will be interesting to keep tabs on; see if they got something there."

The big man stopped speaking for a moment and considered something. Maybe it was the Internet anarchist commune or maybe it was a thought that passed through his mind while talking. In the weeks to come I was to learn how deeply intuitive this man was. He was like some pre-Columbian shaman looking for signs in everything; talking to gods that even his own people had no knowledge of.

"Then there are the more political newsletters. The friendlies include various liberation movements and ecological groups. And of course there's Red Tuesday. She gathers up reports of problems brewing around the world. Dictators rising, infrastructures failing, and the movements of various players in the international killkill games."

"The what?"

"How do you kill a snake?" he asked grabbing me by the arm with a frighteningly quick motion.

I froze and wondered if it was too late to tell him that I didn't want the job.

"Cut off his head," Lawless informed me. "Cut off his head." He let me go and held out his hands in wonder. "To the corporations and former NATO allies this whole world is a nest of vipers. They have units, killkill boys Red Tuesday calls them. These units remove the heads of particularly dangerous vipers. Some of them are well known. You see them on TV and in courtroom cases. Others move like shadows. Red tries to keep tabs on them. She has a special box for the killkill boys and girls just so they know that somebody out there has a machete for their fangs too."

He said this last word like a breathy blast on a toy whistle. It made me laugh.

"Not funny," he told me. "Deadly serious. If you read Red's letters you will know more than any daily papers would ever dare tell you."

I wondered, not for the last time, about my employer's sanity.

"She's crazy of course," Lawless said as though he had read my mind.

"Excuse me?"

"Red. She's crazy. She also has a soap box about the pope. She's had him involved in every conspiracy from that eyeball on the dollar bill to frozen aliens in some Vatican subbasement."

"So how can you trust anything she says?"

"That's just it, son," Lawless said boring those pinpoint eyes into mine. "You can't trust anyone, not completely. But you can't afford not to listen. You have to listen, examine, and then make up your own mind."

The weight of his words settled in on me. It was a way of thinking that produced a paranoia beyond paranoia.

"That sounds like going into the crazy house and asking for commentary on the nightly news," I said, trying to make light of his assertions.

"If the world is insane then you'd be a fool to try and look for sanity to answer the call." Archibald Lawless looked at me with that great heart-shaped face. His bright skin and crown of thorns caused a quickening in my heart.

"The rest of these newsletters and whatnot are from the bad guys. White supremacist groups, pedophile target lists, special memos from certain key international banks. Mostly it's nothing but sometimes it allows you to make a phone call, or something." Again he drifted off into space.

I heard the threat in his voice with that *or something* but by then I knew I had to spend at least a couple of hours with those notes. My aunt Alberta was right about my curiosity. I was always sticking my nose where it didn't belong.

"So you can spend as much time as you want making yourself at home around here. The phone line can be used calling anywhere on the planet but don't use the computer until I show you what's what there." He seemed happy, friendly. He imparted that élan to me. "When you leave just shut the door. It will engage all the locks by it-self, electrically."

As he opened the door to leave my storage office, I asked, "Mr. Lawless?"

"Yeah, son?"

"I don't get it."

"Get what?"

"With all this Red Tuesday, pedophiliac, white supremacist stuff how can you know that you should trust me? I mean all you've done is read some computer files. All that could be forged, couldn't it?"

He smiled and instead of answering my question he said, "You're just like a blank sheet of paper, Orleen. Maybe a name and a date up top but that's all and it's in pencil. You could be my worst nightmare, Felix. But first we've got to get some words down on paper." He smiled again and went out of his office. I followed.

He threw the bolts open and kicked up the buttress. Then he pulled open the door. He made to go out and then thought of some-thing, turned and pointed that teacher's finger at me again.

"Don't open this door for anybody. Not for anyone but me. Don't answer it. Don't say anything through it. You can use this," he tapped a small video monitor that was mounted on the wall to the right of the door, "to see, but that's it."

"W-why?" I stammered.

"The landlord and I have a little dispute going."

"What kind of dispute?"

"I haven't paid rent in seven years and he thinks that it's about time that I did."

"And you don't?"

"The only truth in the bible is where it says that stuff about money and evil," he said and then he hurried out. The door closed behind him, five seconds later the locks all flipped down and the buttress lowered. I noticed then that there was a network of wires that led from the door to a small black box sitting underneath the cushionless couch.

The box was connected to an automobile battery. Even in a blackout Archibald Lawless would have secure doors.

5

I spent that morning inside the mind of a madman or a genius or maybe outside of what Lawless refers to as *the hive mind, the spirit that guides millions of heedless citizens through the aimless acts of everyday life.*

The mess on my office table was a treasure trove of oddities and information. Xeroxed copies of *wanted* posters, guest lists to conservative political fund raisers, blueprints of corporate offices and police stations. Red Tuesday's newsletter had detailed information about the movements of certain *killkills* using their animal code names (like Bear, Ringed Hornet, and Mink). She was less forthcoming about certain saboteurs fighting for anything from ecology to the liberation of so-called political prisoners. For these groups she merely lauded their actions and gave veiled warnings about how close they were to discovery in various cities.

Lawless was right about her and the Catholic Church. She also had a box in each issue surrounded by a border of red and blue crosses in which she made tirades against Catholic crack houses paying for political campaigns and other such absurdities. Even the language was different. This article was the only one that had misspellings and bad grammar.

At the back of every Red Tuesday newsletter, on page four, was an article signed only in the initials AAL. Everything else was written by Red Tuesday. This regular column had a title, REVOLUTIONARY NOTES. After flipping through about fifteen issues I found one column on Archie and the rent.

Never give an inch to the letter of the law if it means submitting to a lie. Your word is your freedom not your bond. If you make a promise, or a promise is made to you, it is imperative that you make sure the word, regardless of what the law says, is upheld. Lies are the basis for all the many crimes that we commit every day. From petty theft to genocide it is a lie that makes it and the truth that settles the account.

Think of it! If only we made every candidate for office responsible for every campaign promise she made. Then you'd see a democracy that hasn't been around for a while. My own landlord promised me whitewashed walls and a red carpet when I agreed to pay his lousy rent. He thought the lie would go down easy, that he could evict me because I never signed a contract. But he had lied. When I took his rooms for month to month he needed the rent and told me that a contract wasn't necessary. He told me that he'd paint and lay carpet, but all that was lies.

It's been years and I'm still here. He hasn't painted or made a cent. I brought him to court and I won. And then, because a man who lies cannot recognize the truth, he sent men to run me out . . .

Never lie and never lie down for a lie. Live according to your word and the world will find its own balance.

I was amazed by the almost innocent and idealistic prattle of such an obviously intelligent man.

The thought of a landlord sending up toughs to run me out of the rooms stopped my lazy reading and sent me out on the job I had been given.

The first person on my list was Valerie Lox. She was a commercial real estate broker on Madison Avenue, just above an exclusive jewelry store. I got there at about eleven forty-five. The offices were small but well appointed. The building was only two floors and the roof had a skylight making it possible for all of the lush green plants to flourish between the three real estate agents' desks.

"Can I help you?" a young Asian man at the desk closest to the door asked.

I suppressed the urge to correct him. *May I*, my mother inside me wanted to say. But I turned my head instead looking out of the window onto posh Madison. Across the street was a furrier, a fancy toy store, and a German pen shop.

"Yes," I said. "I want to see Ms. Lox."

The young man looked me up and down. He didn't like my blue jeans and ratty, secondhand Tibetan sweater—this college wear wasn't designed for Madison Avenue consumption.

"My father is thinking of opening a second office in Manhattan and he wanted me to see what was available," I further explained.

"And your father is?" Another bad sentence.

"JP Orlean of Herman, Bledsoe, and Orlean in New Orleans."

"Wait here." The young man uttered these words, rose from his chair, and walked away.

The two young women agents, one white and the other honey brown, looked from me to the young man as he made his way past them and through a door at the back of the garden room.

I was missing my seminar on the History of the West but that didn't bother me much. I could always get the notes from my friend Claude. And working for Lawless promised to hone my investigative potentials.

"Making sense out of a seemingly incomprehensible jumble of facts." That's what Professor Ortega said at the first lecture I attended at Columbia. His class was called the Art in Article.

I wasn't sure what Lawless was looking for but that didn't worry me. I knew enough from my father's practice to feel safe from involvement in any crime. The test was that even if I went to the police there was nothing concrete I could tell them that they didn't already know.

I was beginning to wonder where the agent had gone when he and a small woman in a dark blue dress came out of the door in back. He veered off and the woman walked straight toward me.

"Mr. Orlean?" she asked with no smile.

"Ms. Lox?" I did smile.

"May I see some form of identification?"

This shocked. When did a real estate agent ask for anything but a deposit? But I took out my wallet and showed her my student ID and Louisiana driver's license. She looked them over carefully and then invited me to follow her into the back.

The head woman's office was no larger than an alcove, there was no skylight or window. Her workstation was a one-piece, salmon pink high school desk next to which sat a short black filing cabinet. She sat and put on a telephone headset, just an earphone and a tiny microphone in front of her mouth.

I stayed standing even though there was a visitor's chair, because I had my manners to maintain.

"Sit," she said, not unkindly.

I did so.

Valerie Lox was a mild blend of contradictions. Her pale skin seemed hard, almost ceramic. Her tightly wound blond hair was in the final phase of turning to white. The hint of yellow was illusive. The face was small and sharp, and her features could have been lightly sculpted and then painted on. Her birdlike body was slender and probably as hard as the rest of her but the blue dress was rich in color and fabric. It was like a royal cloak wrapped around the shoulders of a white twig.

"Why did you need to see my ID?"

"This is an exclusive service, Mr. Orlean," she said with no chink of humanity in her face. "And we like to know exactly who it is we're dealing with."

"Oh," I said. "So it wasn't because of my clothes or my race?"

"The lower races come in all colors, Mr. Orlean. And none of them get back here."

Her certainty sent a shiver down my spine. I smiled to hide the discomfort.

She asked of what assistance she could be to my father. I told her some lies but I forget exactly what. Lying comes easily to me. My aunt Alberta had once told me that lying was a character trait of men on my father's side of the family. That was why they all became lawyers.

"Lawyer even sounds like liar," she used to say. "That's a good thing and it's a bad thing. You got to go with the good, honey chile, no matter what you do."

I spent forty-five minutes looking over photographs and blueprints of offices all over the Madison Avenue area. Nothing cost less than three hundred and fifty thousand a year and Ms. Lox got a whole year's rent as commission. I was thinking maybe I could marry a real estate agent while I worked the paper trade.

Ms. Lox didn't press me. She showed me one office after another asking strategic questions now and then.

"What sort of law would he be practicing?" she asked at one point. "I mean would he need a large waiting room?"

"If he did," I answered, "I wouldn't be here talking to you. Any lawyer with a waiting room is just two steps away from ambulance chasing."

That was the only time I saw her smile.

"Is your father licensed to practice in New York?" she asked at another time.

"You should know," I said.

"Come again?"

"I gave your assistant my father's name and he came back here for five minutes or more. If I were you I would have looked up JP Orlean in the ABA Internet service. There I would have seen that he is not licensed in this state. But you must be aware that he has many clients who have investments and business in the city. A lawyer is mostly mind and a license is easy to rent." These last words were my father's. He used them all the time to out-of-state clients who didn't understand the game.

It struck me as odd that Ms. Lox was so suspicious of me. I was just looking at pictures of commercial spaces. There was nothing top secret that I could steal.

The young Asian man, Brian, brought me an espresso with a coconut cookie while I considered. And when I was through he led me to the front door and said good-bye using my name. I told him, as I had told Valerie Lox, that I would be in touch in a few days after my father and I had a chance to talk.

As I was leaving I saw Valerie Lox standing at the door in back looking after me with something like concern on her porcelain face.

The next stop was a construction site on 23rd Street. Kenneth Cornell, the man I came to see, was some kind of supervisor there. The crew was excavating a deep hole getting ready for the roots of a skyscraper. There were three large cranes moving dirt and stone from the lower depths to awaiting trucks on a higher plane. There was a lot of clanging and whining motors, men, and a few women, shouting, and the impact of hammers, manual and automatic, beating upon the poor New York soil, trying once again to make her submit to their architectural dreams.

I walked in, stated my business, was fitted with a hard hat, and shown into the pit.

They led me to a tin shack half the way down the dirt slope. The man inside the shack was yelling something out of the paneless window at workers looking up from down below. I knew that he was yelling to be heard over the noise but it still gave me the impression that he was a man in a rage. And, being so small, I always stood back when there was rage going on.

Cornell was tall but a bit lanky for construction I thought. His pink chin was partly gray from afternoon shadow and his gray eyes were unsettling because they seemed to look a bit too deeply into my intentions.

"Yeah?"

"Mr. Cornell?"

"Yeah?"

"I'm Orlean," I said pronouncing it *or-leen* as Lawless had done.

"That supposed to mean something to me?"

"I called your office last week—about getting a job," I said.

His eyes tightened, it felt as though they were squeezing my lungs.

"Who are you?" he asked me.

It suddenly occurred to me that I was way out of my depth.

Cornell's hands folded up into fists as if to underscore the epiphany.

"Get the hell out of here," he said.

I didn't exactly run out of that hole but if I had been competing in a walking race I wouldn't have come in last.

6

Lana Drexel, fashion model, was the last name on my list. She was the one I most wanted to see but I didn't make it that day.

Henry Lansman was my second to last stop. He was an easy one, a barber at Crenshaw's, a popular place down in Greenwich Village. There was almost always a line at Crenshaw's. They were an old time barbershop that catered to the conservative thirty-something crowd. They gave classic haircuts in twelve minutes and so could afford to undercut, so to speak, the competition.

The shop, I knew from friends, had nine barber chairs that were all busy all of the time. But because this was a Tuesday at two-thirty there were only about ten or twelve customers waiting in line at the top of the stairwell of the shop. You had to go down a half flight of stairs to get into the establishment. I can't say what the inside of the place looked like because I never made it there.

"Hey," someone said in tone that was opening to fear. "Hey, mister."

"Excuse me," a man in a red parka said before he shouldered me aside hard enough to have thrown me down the stairwell if there hadn't been a portly gentleman there to block my fall.

"Hey, man! What the fuck!" the big man I fell against hollered. He was wearing some kind of blue uniform.

I wanted to see who it was that pushed me. I did catch a glimpse of the top of the back of his head. It had partly gray close-cut hair. He was crouching down and the parka disguised his size, and, anyway, the big guy I slammed into needed an apology.

"I'm sorry . . ." I said and then the shouting started.

"Hey, mister. Mister! Hey I think this guy's havin' a heart attack!"

The big man had put his hand on my shoulder but the terror in the crackling tone distracted him long enough for me to rush to the side of the young man who was screaming. I wish I could say that it was out of concern for life that moved me so quickly but I really just wanted to save myself from being hit.

The screamer was a white man, tall and well built. He was tan and wore an unbuttoned black leather jacket and a coal colored loose-knit shirt that was open at the neck revealing a thick gold chain that hung around his throat. He had a frightened child's eyes. His fear was enough to convince me to clear out before the danger he saw could spread. I would have run away if it wasn't for the dying man at my feet.

I crouched down on one knee to get a closer look at the heart attack victim. There was a fleck of foam at the corner of his mouth. The lips were dark, the panic in his wide eyes was fading into death. He wore a short-sleeved nylon shirt which was odd because this was late October and on the chilly side. His gray slacks rode a little high. He was almost completely bald.

The struggle in his eyes was gone by the time I had noticed these things. I cradled the back of his head with my hand. A spasm went through his neck. His back arched and I thought he was trying to rise. But then he slumped back down. Blood seeped out of his left nostril.

"He's dead," the someone whispered.

Men and women all around were voicing their concern but I only made out one sentence, "Mr. Bartoli, it's Henry, Henry Lansman!" a man's voice shouted.

I was watching the color drain from the dead man's face thinking that I should clear out or tell somebody what I knew. But all I could do was kneel there holding the heavy head, watching the drop of blood making its way down his jowl.

"Out of the way! Let him go!" a man ordered.

A round man, hard from muscle, pushed me aside. He was wearing a white smock. At first I thought it was a doctor. But then I realized it must be someone from the barbershop.

I moved aside and kept on going. The screamer with the gold chain was leaning against the window of the shoe store next door. His tan had faded. I remember thinking that some poor woman would have to have sex with him all night long before the color came back.

Henry Lansman was dead. People were shouting for someone to call an ambulance. I stayed watching until I heard the first far-off whine of the siren then I walked away from the scene feeling guilty though not knowing why.

I went over to Saint Mark's Place, a street filled with head shops, twelve-step programs, and wild youths with punk hair and multiple piercings. There was a comic book store that I frequented and a quasi-Asian restaurant that was priced for the college student pocketbook.

I ordered soba noodles with sesame sauce and a triple espresso. I finished the coffee but only managed about half of the entrée. I sat there thinking about the ceramic woman, the angry man, and the dead barber. That morning I was just a college student looking for a job. By afternoon I had witnessed a man dying.

I considered my options. The first one was calling my father. He knew lawyers in New York. Good ones. If I told him what was wrong he'd be on the next plane. JP would be there. He'd body block anyone trying to hurt me. He'd do anything to save me from danger. But then he'd take me back down to Louisiana and tell me how stupid I was and which law school I was to attend. He might even tell me that I had to live at home for a while.

And how could I say no if I begged him to save me?

And anyway it looked like a heart attack that killed Lansman. I decided that I was just being oversensitive to the paranoia of Lawless and Red Tuesday.

The man was just sick.

"Didn't you like it?" the slightly overweight, blue-haired, black waitress asked. Actually her hair was brown with three bright blue streaks running back from her forehead.

"I like you," I said, completely out of character.

She gave me a leery look and then walked away to the kitchen. She returned with my bill a few moments later. At the bottom was her telephone number and her name, Sharee.

I called Lawless's answering machine from a pay phone on the street.

"Lox and Cornell are fine," I said after the tone. "But Lansman died of a heart attack. He fell dead just when I got there. I didn't get to Drexel and I quit too. You don't have to pay me."

From there I went up to the special lab room that was set up for us at Columbia. There were three computers that were connected to AP, UPI, and Reuters news databases. There were also lines connected to police and hospital reports in Manhattan. Lansman's death wasn't even listed. That set my mind at ease some. If there was no note of his death it had to be some kind of medical problem and not foul play.

I followed breaking news in the Middle East and Africa until late that night. There had been a car bomb near the presidential residence in Caracas, Venezuela. I wondered, briefly, what Red Tuesday would have made of that.

It was midnight by the time I got to 121st Street. I made it to our apartment house, the Madison, and climbed six floors. I was walking down the hall when a tall man in a dark suit appeared before me.

"Mr. Orlean?"

"Yes?"

"We need to speak to you."

"It's late," I complained and then made to walk around him.

He moved to block my way.

Backing up I bumped into something large and soft so I turned. Another obstacle in the form of a man in a suit stood before me.

The first man was white, the second light brown.

"We need to talk to you at the station," the brown man informed me.

"You're the police?"

Instead of speaking he produced a badge.

"What do you want with me?" I asked, honestly confused. I had put my dealings with Archibald Lawless that far behind me.

"You're a witness to a possible crime," the man behind me said.

I turned and looked at him. He had a big nose with blue and red veins at the surface. His breath carried the kind of halitosis that you had to take pills for.

The brown man pulled my arms behind my back and clapped handcuffs on my wrists.

"You don't arrest witnesses," I said.

"You've been moving around a lot, son," the white cop said, exhaling a zephyr of noxious fumes. "And we need to know some answers before we decide if we're going to charge you with something or not."

"Where's your warrant?" I said in a loud voice intended to waken my roommate. But I was cut short by the quick slap from the man I came to know as August Morganthau.

7

They took me to the 126th Street station. There were police cars parked up and down the block. I was taken past a waiting room full of pensive looking citizens. They weren't manacled or guarded so I figured they were there to make complaints or to answer warrants. I *was* a felon in their eyes, cuffed and manhandled, shoved past them like a thief.

They took me to a Plexiglas booth where a uniformed officer filled out what I came to know later as an entry slip.

"Name?" the sentry asked.

I was looking at the floor to avoid the nausea caused by Morganthau's breath.

"Name?"

I realized that I was expected to answer the question. It seemed unfair. Why should I tell him my name? I didn't ask to be there.

"Felix Orlean," I said taking great pleasure in withholding my middle names.

"Middle name?"

I shook my head.

"Case number?"

"I don't know," I said, trying now to be helpful. I regretted the childish withholding of my name.

"Of course you don't, stupid," Morganthau said. He shoved me too.

"Case six-three-two-two-oh, homicide," the chubby brown man, Tito Perez, said.

"Charges?"

"Pending," Officer Morganthau grunted.

There was a Plexiglas wall next to the booth with a rude door cut into it. The edges were all uneven and it had only a makeshift wire hanger handle. I got the impression that one day the police realized that if someone got loose with a gun there would be a lot of casualties unless they put up a bulletproof barrier between them and the phantom shooter. So they bought some used Plexiglas and cut it into walls and doors and whatnot. After that they never thought about it again.

Perez pulled open the door. It wasn't locked, couldn't be as far as I could see. They pushed me along an aisle of cubicles. Men and women wearing headsets were sitting behind the low-cut walls talking to the air or each other. Some of them were in uniform, some not. Mostly it was women. Almost all of them white. The room was shabby. The carpet under my feet was worn all the way to the floor in places. The cubicles were piled high with folders, scraps of pink and white papers, coffee cups, and small heaps of sweaters, shirts, and caps. The tan cubicle walls weren't all straight. A few were missing, some were half rotted away or stained from what must have been water damage of some sort.

If this was the nerve center of police intelligence for that neighborhood, crime was a good business opportunity to consider.

I see how slipshod the police seemed now. But that night, while I merely recorded what I saw with my eyes, my mind was in a state of full-blown horror. As soon as I got to a phone I was going to call my father's twenty-four-hour service. Betty was the woman on the late night shift. She'd get to him no matter where he was.

We reached a large cubicle that was not only disheveled but it also smelled. The smell was sharp and unhealthy. Morganthau sat down on one of a pair of gray steel desks that faced each other. He indicated the chair that sat at the desk for me.

"Can you take these things off my hands?" I asked.

"Sorry," he said with an insincere gray smile. "Policy."

I lifted my arms to go behind the back of the chair and sat slightly hunched over.

"I'm Morganthau and this is Officer Perez," he said. "Tell us what you know about Hank Lansman."

The "Hank" threw me off for a second. I frowned trying to connect it.

"Come on, kid," Perez said. "You were seen at the barbershop. We know you were there."

My mind flooded with thoughts. How did they know I was there? Was Lansman murdered? Even if someone saw me how would they know my name? I didn't tell anyone. I don't have a record or even any friends in that part of town.

All of this was going on just barely in the range of consciousness. Most of what I felt was fear and discomfort. Morganthau's breath was beginning to reach my nostrils again. That coupled with the sharp odor of the cubicle started to seriously mess with my stomach.

"I want to make a phone call."

"Later," Perez said. His voice was soft.

"I have a right . . ." I began but I stopped when Morganthau put his shod foot, sole down, on my lap.

"I asked you a question," he said.

"A man named Archibald Lawless hired me to see about four people. He didn't tell me why." I gave them the names of Lox, Lansman, Drexler, and Cornell. "He said that I should go see these people, make sure I saw them in the flesh."

"And then what?"

"That's all he said. He said see them. I suppose he wanted me to make a report but we didn't get that far."

"What were you supposed to say to these people when you saw them?" Perez asked.

"What was said didn't matter. Just make sure I saw them, that's all. Listen. I don't know anything about this. I answered an ad in the paper. It was for Lawless. He said that he wanted a scribe . . ."

"We know all about Lawless," Morganthau said. "We know about his *scribes* and we know about you too."

"There's nothing about me that has to do with him."

"One dead man," Perez suggested.

"I thought he had a heart attack?"

The officers looked at each other.

"We don't need any shit, kid," Morganthau said. "Who else is in the cell?"

It was at that moment I began to fear that even my father could not save me.

I had to swallow twice before saying, "What do you mean?"

Morganthau's foot was still in my lap. He increased the weight a little and said, "This is about to get ugly."

I felt cold all of a sudden. My head was light and my tongue started watering.

"Shit!" Morganthau shouted. He pulled his foot back from my thighs but not before I vomited soba noodles all over his pant leg. "Damn!"

He skipped away. Perez flung open a drawer in his desk and threw a towel to his partner who began wiping his pants as he went back down the corridor we came from.

"You're in trouble now, kid," Perez said.

If I had seen it on a TV show I would have sneered at the weak dialogue. But in that chair I was scared to death. I retched twice more and steeled my neck to keep from crying.

After he was sure that I was through being sick, Perez jerked me up by the arm and dragged me down another corridor until we came to a big room where there were other chained prisoners. All of them male.

The center of the room was empty of furniture except for a small table in the middle of the floor where a lone sentry sat. Along three walls ran metal benches that were bolted to the floor. Every four feet or so along each bench there was a thick eyebolt also planted in the concrete floor. There were three eyebolts along each bench. Six men were attached to these stations by manacles that also held their feet. All of these men were negroes.

"Finney," Perez said. "Grab me some bracelets for this one."

Finney was my age with pale strawberry hair. He was tall and long limbed. He had to stand up in order to kneel down and reach under the table for the restraints. Perez undid my handcuffs, made me sit at a station next to a big brown man who was rocking backward and forth and talking to himself. He was smiling through his words, which were mostly indistinct, and tapping his right foot on the concrete. Two places away, on the other side was a man so big that it didn't seem as if the chains he wore could possibly hold him. Across the way was a young, very mean looking man. All he wore was a pair of tattered jeans. His eyes bored into mine. It was as if I were his worst enemy and finally my throat was within his reach.

Perez didn't say anything to me or even look me in the face. He simply attached the new manacles to my ankles and wrists and secured the chains to the eyebolt in the floor. Then he went to fill out a form on Finney's table. After they exchanged words, which I couldn't make out, Perez left through the door we had entered.

8

I was relieved to be away from Morganthau's putrid breath. At least I had a few moments to think about what happened so far. If Lansman was murdered the man in the red parka had something to do with it. I wanted to tell the police about him but they seemed so sure of my guilt that I thought they might construe any information I gave them as confirmation of my culpability. I wasn't very experienced with police procedure but I knew a lot about the law from my father and grandfather, LJ Orlean.

I knew that I needed to speak to a lawyer before I could have any kind of meaningful dialogue with the law. But they didn't seem ready to allow me my Constitutional phone call. I was screwing up my courage to ask the midwestern looking Finney for my one call when the big guy two spaces to my left began speaking to me.

"You look like a cherry," he said. It was almost a question.

"Cherry, cherry, cherry . . ." the grinning rocker on the other side chanted.

"You might need a friend," the big man suggested.

"I'm all right," I said with nary a break in my voice.

". . . cherry, cherry, cherry . . ."

"You dissin' me, bitch?" the big man asked, this time it was hardly a question.

I didn't know what to say. An apology seemed inappropriate and getting down on my knees to beg was not what a man should do in such a situation.

The man across from me mouthed a sentence that was either announcing his intention of killing or kissing me, I didn't know which.

"Officer," I said. "Officer."

". . . cherry, cherry, cherry, cherry . . ."

"Officer."

"Shut up," Finney said.

"Officer, I haven't been given the right to a phone call yet. I want to make that call now."

The strawberry blond didn't respond. He was reading something. I honestly believe that he no longer heard me.

"I'ma bust you up, punk," the big man to my left proclaimed.

I started thinking about the possibility of weapons at my disposal. *A man is only as strong as his th'oat or his groin.* My aunt Alberta's words came back to me with a flash of heat and then cold passing over my scalp. *Just remember, baby—don't hesitate, not for a minute.*

". . . cherry, cherry . . ."

I glanced at the big man. He had fists the width of a small tree's trunk. I decided that when I got the chance I'd go in low on him: hit him hard and ruin him for life. Jail had turned me into a felon and I hadn't been there an hour.

A phone rang, which in itself was not unusual but I couldn't see a phone anywhere in the room. It rang again.

". . . cherry, cherry, I want some," the rocking man sang.

The shirtless man across the way was still mouthing his violent flirtation.

The phone rang for the third time.

The guard turned the page of his magazine.

The big man on the left suddenly yanked on his chains with all his might. My heart leapt. I was sure that he'd break those flimsy shackles.

"Settle down, Trainer," the blond guard said. Then he got up and walked to the wall where there was a space between the benches.

The phone rang.

"You gonna suck my toes, niggah," the man called Trainer promised.

The kid across the way made me another promise.

The phone rang. The room started spinning. The guard located a hidden door in the wall and pulled it open. He reached in and came out with a yellow phone receiver connected to a black cord.

"Finney here," he said.

". . . cherry, cherry the best dessert," the rocking man said. "Cherry, cherry in the dirt."

Maybe he didn't say those words but that's what I remember. The room was spinning and my sweater smelled of vomit. Finney looked at me.

". . . cherry . . ."

". . . suck on my big black dick . . ."

". . . Orlean?" Finney said.

"What?"

"Are you Felix Orlean?" he asked.

"Yes sir."

"*Yes sir,*" Trainer said. He was trying to make fun of me but I think he realized that I might soon be beyond his reach.

"He's here," Finney said into the receiver.

He hung up the phone and went back to his chair and magazine.

"Hm," Trainer said. "Looks like they just wanted to make sure you was up here wit' me."

"Fuck you," I said. I didn't mean to, I really didn't. But I was sick and he was stupid . . .

"What did you say?"

"I said, fuck you, asshole."

Trainer's eyes widened. The veins on his neck were suddenly engorged with blood. His lips actually quivered. And then I did the worst thing I could have done to such a man—I laughed.

What did I have to lose? He was going to brutalize me if he could anyway. Maybe I could catch him by the nuts like my aunt Alberta had advised.

"You a dead man," Trainer promised.

"Mash his cherry, Jerry," the rocking man tapped his toe for each syllable.

I lowered my head and tried to remember the Lord's prayer.

I could not.

Then I heard the door to the strange room open. I looked up to see a white man walking through. He was tall and dressed in an expensive gray suit.

"Which one is Orlean?" the white man asked Blondie.

"Over there." Finney gestured with his chin.

"Unlock him."

"Rules are you need two guards to remove a recal," the guard replied.

"Get up off your ass, kid, or I will have you mopping up vomit in the drunk tank for a month of Sundays." The gray suit had a deadly certain voice.

The guard got up and unlocked my fetters. I stood up and smiled at Trainer and the shirtless man across the way.

"This way, Felix," the man in the gray suit said.

"I'm gonna remember you, Felix Orlean," the prisoner Trainer said.

"Whatever you say, loser," I said smiling. "Maybe you'll learn something."

Again the prisoner named Trainer strained at his bonds. He jumped at me but there was no give to his chains. I was scared to death. The only way I kept from going crazy was taunting my helpless tormentor.

The man in the gray suit took me by the shoulder and guided me out of the room. The shirtless detainee spat on the floor as I left. Trainer screeched like a mad elephant.

We walked down a long corridor coming to a small elevator at last. The car went up seven floors and opened into a room that was almost livable. There were carpets and stuffed chairs and the smell of decent coffee.

"You can go in there and clean up," the suit said, pointing toward a closed door.

"What's your name?" I asked him.

"Captain Delgado."

The door led to a large restroom and shower area. I took off my college clothes and got under a spigot for at least fifteen minutes. After the shower I washed the vomit from my sweater. Between the lateness of the hour, the heat, dehydration, and fear I was so tired that it was hard to keep moving.

I staggered back to the room where Delgado waited. He was sitting in a big red chair, reading a newspaper.

"Feel better?"

"Uh-huh."

"Let's go then."

We retraced every step I'd taken through the station. Me sticking close to the slick policeman and him leading the way. Nobody stopped us, nobody questioned our passing.

We went to a '98 Le Sabre parked out in front of the station and Delgado drove us up further into Harlem.

"Where we going?" I asked.

"Up on One Fifty-sixth," he said.

"I'd like to go home."

"No you wouldn't. Take my word on that."

"What's going on, Captain?"

"I haven't the slightest idea, son."

We stopped in front of a large stone apartment building on 156th Street. Even though it was late there were young men and women hanging out around the front stoop.

"Eight twenty-one," Delgado said.

"What?"

"Apartment eight twenty-one. That's where you're going."

"I want to go home."

"Get out."

"Are you coming?"

"No."

I had never felt more vulnerable in my life.

I opened the door and all the faces from the stoop turned toward me.

"Who's up there?" I asked Delgado.

He pulled my door shut and drove off.

"You a cop, man?" a young man asked me.

He had climbed down from his seat on the top step of the stoop.

"No. No. He just gave me a ride."

My inquisitor was probably a year or two younger than I. His skin was very dark. Even though the air was chilly he wore only a T-shirt. His arms were slender but knotty with muscle.

"You fuckin' wit' me, man?"

"No. I'm supposed to go to an apartment upstairs."

Two other angry looking youths climbed down from the stoop. They flanked my interlocutor, searching me with their eyes.

"What for?" the youth asked.

"They told me that the man who had me released is up there."

I started walking. I had to go around my three new friends. Up the stoop I went and into the dark corridor of the first floor.

There was no light and I could almost feel the young men they followed me so closely. As we climbed the stairs they spoke to me.

"You with the cops you ain't gonna get outta here, mothah-fuckah," one of them said.

"We should take him now, Durkey," another suggested.

"Let's see where he go," Durkey, the first one who had approached me, said. "Let's check it out."

I was breathing hard by the time I got to the eighth floor landing. Most of the journey was made through semi-darkness. Along the way there was some light from open apartment doors. Silent sentinels came to mark our passing: children, old people, women, and some men. But no one asked Durkey and his henchmen why they were following me.

I had been in places like this before, in the Ninth Ward, New Orleans. But I was always under the protection of my aunt Alberta and her boyfriends. Being from a light-skinned family of the upper crust of colored society I was always seen as an outsider.

I knocked on the door to apartment eight twenty-one and waited—and prayed.

"Nobody there," Durkey said.

He put a hand on my shoulder.

The door opened flooding the hallway with powerful light. I winced. Durkey's hand fled my shoulder.

Archibald Lawless appeared in the doorway.

"Mr. Madison," he said loudly. "I see that you've accompanied my guest upstairs."

"Hey, Lawless," Durkey said with deference. "I didn't know he was your boy."

"Uh-huh," the anarchist said. "You can go now."

My retinue of toughs backed away. My recent, and ex, boss smiled.

"Come on in, Felix. You've had a busy day."

9

It was an opulent room. The floors were covered in thick, rose-colored carpets. On the walls hung a dozen eighteenth century paintings of countrysides and beautiful young men and women of all races. There was a fireplace with a gas blaze raging and a large dark-wood table set with cheeses, meats, fruits, and bottles of wine.

"Have a seat," Lawless said.

There was a big backless couch upholstered with the rough fur of bear or maybe beaver.

"What's going on?" I asked.

"Are you hungry?"

"I don't know. I threw up at the police station."

"Wine then," Archibald said. He took a dark green bottle and a slender water glass from the table. He filled the glass halfway with the dark red liquid and handed it to me.

It was the finest burgundy I'd ever tasted. Rich, fruity, almost smoky.

"Cheese?" Lawless asked.

"In a minute," I said. "Is this your apartment?"

"I own the building," he said blandly. "Bought it when the prices were still depressed."

"You're a landlord?"

"Building manager is the title I prefer. I collect a certain amount of rent from my tenants until they've paid for the cost of their unit. After that they pay whatever maintenance is necessary for taxes and upkeep."

I must have been gaping at him.

"It's the way Fidel does it in Cuba," he said.

"Castro's a dictator."

"And Bush is a democratically elected official," he replied.

"But . . ." I said.

Lawless held up his hand.

"We'll have enough time to discuss politics on slow days at the office," he said. "Right now we have some more pressing business."

I'd drunk the half glass and he replenished it.

"I left you a message," I said. "Did you get it?"

"Tell me about the murder," he replied.

"But I quit."

"No."

The wine felt good in my belly and in my blood. It warmed me and slowed the fear I'd felt since being taken by the police. I was safe, even hidden, with a man who seemed to be a force of nature all on his own. His refusal to accept my resignation made me tired. I took another swig, sat the glass down on an antique wooden crate used as a table, and let my head loll backward.

"I'm not working for you," I said. And then my eyes closed. I forced them open but couldn't keep focus. I closed my eyes again and I must have fallen asleep for a while.

The next thing I knew there was somebody whimpering somewhere . . .

"Ohhhhh the wolverines. The maggots and the ticks. Blood suckers and whores . . ."

The voice was high which somehow fit with the headache threaded behind my eyes. I sat up and regretted it. My stomach was still unsteady, my tongue dry as wood.

". . . whores and pimps and teachers sticking sticks in your ass . . ."

Lawless was rolling on the floor, whining out these complaints. At first I thought he must have had too much wine. I went to him, touched his shoulder.

He rose under me like the ground in a terrible upheaval. Grabbing me by my hair and right shoulder he lifted me high above the floor.

"Don't you fuck with me, mother fucker!" he shouted.

His small eyes were almost large with the fear.

"It's me, Mr. Lawless," I said. "Felix. Your scribe."

He lowered me slowly, painfully because of his hold on my hair.

"I'm sick," he cried when he'd released me. "Sick."

He swayed left then right and then fell in a heap like a young child in despair. I looked around the room for something that might help him. I didn't see anything so I took a doorway that led me into a master bedroom painted dark blue with a giant bed in the center. There was a skylight in this room. Light came in from an outside source somewhere. There was a white bag on the bed made from the skin of what seemed to be an albino crocodile. You had to open the mouth and reach in past the sharp teeth to see what was inside. Therein I found a knife and pistol, an English bible and an old copy of the Koran in both English and Arabic. There was a clear plastic wallet filled with one-dollar bills and a small amber vial which contained a dozen or so tiny tablets.

There was no label on the glass tube.

Archibald Lawless had stripped off his clothes by the time I returned to the living room. He was squatting down and rocking not unlike the man in the police station.

I knelt down next him, held up the small bottle, and asked, "How many do you take, Mr. Lawless?"

His eyes opened wide again.

"Who are you?"

"Felix Orlean, your scribe. You hired me yesterday."

"Are you killkill?"

"I'm not on any of Red Tuesday's lists."

For some reason this made him laugh. He took the bottle from me and dumped all the pills in his mouth. He chewed them up and said, "I better get into the bed before I go unconscious—or dead."

I helped him into the bedroom. I think he was asleep before his head hit the mattress.

For the next few hours I hung around the big bed. Lawless was unconscious but fitful. He talked out loud in his sleep speaking in at least four different languages. I understood the Spanish and German but the other dialects escaped me. Most of his utterances were indistinct. But his tone was plaintive enough that I could feel the pain.

Now and then I went back into the living room. I had some

cheddar and a sip of burgundy. After a while I started putting the food away in the kitchen, which was through a door opposite the bedroom entrance.

I stayed because I was afraid to leave. The police might still be after me for all I knew. Delgado seemed to owe a debt to Lawless but that didn't mean that Perez and Morganthau wouldn't grab me again. And somehow I'd been implicated in a murder. I had to know what was going on.

But there was more to it than that. The self-styled anarchist seemed so helpless when I'd come to. His mental state was definitely unstable and he did get me out of jail. I felt that I should wait, at least until he was aware and able to take care of himself.

There was a bookshelf in the bathroom. The books were composed of two dominant genres: politics and science fiction. I took out a book entitled *Soul of the Robot* by the author Barrington J. Bayley. It was written in the quick style of pulp fiction, which I liked because there was no pretension to philosophy. It was just a good story with incredible ideas.

I'd been reading on the bear or beaver couch for some while when there came a knock on the front door. Five quick raps and then silence. I didn't even take a breath.

I counted to three and the knock came again.

Still I didn't make a sound.

I might have stayed there silently, breathing only slightly. But then the doorknob jiggled.

I moved as quietly as I could toward the door.

"Who is it?" I called.

The doorknob stopped moving.

"Who is that?" a woman's voice asked.

"I'm Felix. I work for Mr. Lawless."

"Open the door, Felix." Her voice was even and in charge.

"Who are you?"

"My name is Maddie. I need to see Archie." A sweetness came into her voice.

I tried to open the door but there were three locks down the side that required specialized attention. One had a knob in a slot shaped like a simple maze. The next one had a series of three buttons that needed to be pressed.

"Are you going to let me in, Felix?" Maddie asked.

"Trying to get the locks."

The last lock was a bolt. The knob was on a spring that allowed it be pushed in. I squashed the knob inward but the bolt refused to slide. I tried pulling it out but that didn't work either.

"Felix?"

"I'm trying."

The hand on my shoulder made me jump into the door.

"What's wrong?" Maddie asked from her side.

"Nothing, M," Archibald Lawless said from behind me.

"Archie," the woman called.

"Meet me at Sunshine's at noon," Lawless said to the door, his hand still on my shoulder.

"Will you be there?" she asked.

"Absolutely. I can't let you in right now because I'm in the middle of something, something I have to finish."

"You promise to meet me," the disembodied woman said.

"You have my word."

He had on camouflage pants and a black T-shirt, black motorcycle boots and a giant green inlaid ring on the point finger of his left hand.

"Okay," Maddie said.

I inhaled deeply.

"You've got the job," he said.

10

Lawless drank a glass of wine, said, "Sleep on the couch," and stumbled back toward his bedroom.

I lay down not expecting to sleep a wink but the next thing I knew there was sunlight coming through a window and the smell of food in the air. There was a small table at the far end of the narrow kitchen. The chairs set there looked out of a window, down on the playground of an elementary school. He made griddle cakes with a sweet pecan sauce, spicy Andouille sausage, and broiled grapefruit halves with sugar glazed over the top, set off by a few drops of bourbon.

I tried to ask him questions while he was cooking but he put them all off asking me instead about parts of New Orleans that I knew well.

I loved talking about my city. The music and the food, the racial diversity and the fact that it was the only really French city in the United States.

"I used to go down there a lot," Lawless told me while flipping our cakes. "Not to the city so much as the swamplands. There's some people out around there who live like human beings."

When the breakfast was finally served he sat down across from me. There was a girl in the asphalt yard calling up to her mother in some apartment window. I couldn't discern what they were saying because I was studying the madman's eyes.

"I have a few disorders," he said after passing a hand over his food.

"You mean about last night?"

"Bipolar, mildly schizophrenic," he continued. "One doctor called it a recurring paranoid delusional state but I told him that if he had seen half the things that I have that he'd live in Catatonia and eat opium to wake up."

His laugh was only a flash of teeth and a nod. Everything Lawless did seemed pious and sacred—though I was sure he did not believe in God.

"Are you under a doctor's care?" I asked him.

"You might say that," he said. "I have a physician in New Delhi. A practitioner of ancient lore. He keeps me stocked with things like those pills you fed me. He keeps the old top spinning."

Lawless pointed at his head.

"Maybe you're addicted," I suggested.

"Tell me about the murder," he replied.

"I'm not working for you."

"Are you going to work for yourself?" he asked.

"What does that mean?"

"It means that it would be in your best interest to give me the information you have. That way I can make sure that the police and anybody else will leave you alone."

He was right of course. But I didn't want to admit it. I felt as if I had been tricked into my problems and I blamed A. Lawless for that.

"First I want *you* to answer some questions," I said.

Lawless smiled and held his palms up—as in prayer.

"Who was that guy in the green suit talking about in your office yesterday?" I asked.

"A diamond dealer named Benny Lamarr. He was from South Africa originally but he relocated to New York about five years ago."

"Why did you want to know about him?"

Lawless smiled. Then he nodded.

"I have a friend in the so-called intelligence center here in New York. She informs me when the government takes an interest in the arrests, detainments, deaths, or in the liberation of citizens, aliens, and government officials."

"This is someone in your employ?" I asked.

"In a manner of speaking. I maintain Nelly, but she only gives me information that is, or should be, public record. You know, Felix, the government and big business hide behind a mountain of data. They hide, in plain sight, the truth from us. I tease out that truth so that at least one man knows what's going on."

"What did this Nelly tell you?" I asked.

"The diamond dealer died in an automobile accident. There was no question of foul play on the local level but still the death was covered up. His files were sealed and sent to Arizona."

"Arizona?"

"There's a government facility outside of Phoenix where certain delicate information is handled."

"Did you know this Lamarr?" I asked.

"No."

"Then why are you so concerned with him?"

"When I looked into Lamarr's past I found that he had recently been seen in the company of a man named Tellman Drake. Drake had also moved to New York and changed his name to Kenneth Cornell. When I looked into both men together I found the other names on our list."

"So what?"

Archibald Lawless smiled.

"What are you grinning about?" I asked him.

"You're good at asking questions," he said. "That's a fine trait and something to know about you."

"You're only going to know me long enough to get me out of this trouble you started."

Lawless held up his palms again. "Lamarr was in diamonds. Valerie Lox leases expensive real estate around the world. Tellman Drake—"

"Kenneth Cornell," I said to make sure that I was following the story.

"Yes," the anarchist said. "Kenny Cornell is a world class demolitions expert. Henry Lansman was an assassin when he lived in

Lebanon, and Lana Drexel . . . Well, Lana Drexel learned when she was quite young that men, and women too, would give up their most guarded secrets in the light of love."

"And the government was looking into all of these people?"

"I'm looking into them."

"Why?"

"Because Lamarr's murder was covered up."

"You said it was an accident."

"The facts were smothered, sent to Arizona," Lawless said. "That's enough for me."

"Enough for you to what?"

"Walk the line."

The words chilled me in spite of my conviction to treat Lawless as an equal.

"Are you working for someone?" I managed to ask.

"For everyone. For the greater good," Lawless said. "But now I've answered your questions. You tell me what happened when you saw Henry Lansman die."

"One more question." I said.

"Okay."

"Who is Captain Delgado to you?"

"An ambitious man. Not a man to trust but someone to be used. He wants to advance in the department and he knows that I have a reach far beyond his own. We get together every month or so. I point him where I might need some assistance and, in return, he answers when I call."

"It all sounds very shady."

"I need you, Felix," Archibald Lawless said then. "I need someone who can ask questions and think on his feet. Stick with me a day or two. I'll pay you and I'll make sure that all the problems that have come up for you will be gone."

"What is it that you're asking me to do?" I asked.

I thought I was responding to his offer of exoneration. But now, when I look back, I wonder if maybe it wasn't his unashamed admission of need that swayed me.

"Tell me about the death of Henry Lansman," he said for the third time.

I gave him every detail I remembered down to the waitress and the half-eaten meal.

"We need to talk to at least one of these players," Lawless said. "I want to know what's going on."

"Which one?"

"Lana Drexel I should think," he said. "Yes definitely Lana . . ."

He stood up from the table and strode back toward the living room. I followed. From under the fur divan he pulled a slender brief-case. When he opened it, I could see that it contained twenty amber colored bottles in cozy velvet insets.

"These are the medicines that Dr. Meta has prescribed for me. Here . . ." From the upper flap of the briefcase he pulled three sheets of paper that were stapled together. "These are the instructions about what chemical I need in various manifest states. This last bottle is an aerosol spray. You might need it to subdue me in case my mind goes past reason."

"You want me to tote this around behind you?"

"No," he said. "I just want you to see it. I have a variety of these bags. If I start slipping all I need is for you to help me out a little."

Hearing his plea I felt a twinge of emotion and then the suspicion that Archibald Lawless was messing with my mind.

11

"Lana Drexel," the anarchist was saying to me a while later. We were having a glass of fresh lemonade that he'd prepared in the kitchen. "She's the most dangerous of the whole bunch."

"What do you mean?"

"Valerie Lox or Kenny Cornell are like nine-year-old hall guards compared to her."

"She's the smallest," I said, "and the youngest."

"She swallows down whole men three times her age and weight," Lawless added. "But she's fair to look at and you're only young once no matter how long you live."

"Are you going to your meeting?" I asked him.

"What meeting?"

"The one with the woman you talked to through the door."

"Oh no," he said, shaking his head. "No. Never. Not me."

———

I was thinking about our conversation when I entered the Rudin apartment building on East 72nd.

Lawless had given me one of his authentic Afghan sweaters to make up for the sweater I vomited on. I looked a little better than I had before but not good enough to saunter past the doorman at Lana Drexel's building.

"Yes?" the sentry asked. He wore a dark blue coat festooned with dull brass buttons, a pair of pale blue pants with dark stripes down the side, and light blue gloves.

"Drexel," I said.

The doorman—who was also a white man and a middle-aged man—sneered.

"And your name is?" he asked as if he expected me to say, *Mud*.

"Lansman," I replied smugly. "Henry Lansman."

The doorman reached into his glass alcove-office and pulled out a phone receiver. He pressed a few digits on the stem, waited and then said, "A Mr. Lansman."

It was a pleasure to see his visage turn even more sour. I think, when he looked to me that he was still half inclined to turn me away.

"Back elevator," he said. "Twenty-fifth floor."

"What's the apartment number?" I asked.

"It's the only door," he said getting at least some pleasure out of my naiveté.

The elevator was small but well-appointed, lined with rosewood, floored in plush maroon carpeting, and lit by a tasteful crystal chandelier. The doors slid opened revealing a small red room, opposite a pink door. This door was held ajar by a small olive-skinned woman who had eyes twice the size they should have been. Her hair was thick, bronze and golden of color. Her cheekbones were high and her chin just a shade lower than where you might have expected it to be. She was beautiful the way the ocean is beautiful. Not a human charm that you could put your arms around but all the exquisiteness of a wild orchid or a distant explosion. It was a cold beauty that you knew was burning underneath. But there was no warmth or comfort in the pull of Lana Drexel's magnetism. There was only a jungle and, somewhere in the thickness of that hair, a tiger's claws.

She looked me up and down with and said, "You're not Lansman."

"Sorry," I said. "But he's dead."

I had practiced that line for two hours. Lawless had given me the job of getting in to see the fashion model and of convincing her to come to his office and share what she knew about the other names on his list. It was my idea to pretend that I was the dead man. I also decided that shock might loosen her tongue.

But if she was in any way alarmed I couldn't see it.

"He is?" she said.

"Yeah. The people around thought that it was a heart attack but then the police arrested me and said something about murder."

"So he was murdered?" she asked.

"I thought I'd come here and ask you."

"Why?"

"Because the police for some reason suspect me of being involved with you guys and your business. You see, I'm just a journalism student and I'd like them to leave me alone."

"Excuse me," she said, still holding the door against my entrée, still unperturbed by the seriousness of our talk, "but what is your real name?"

It was her turn to frighten me. I thought that if she was to know my name then she could send someone after me. I lamented, not for the last time, agreeing to work for the anarchist.

"I'm a representative of Archibald Lawless," I said, "Anarchist at large."

Lana Drexel's confident expression dissolved then. She fell back allowing the door to come open. She wandered into the large room behind her.

I followed.

I began to think that you could understand the strange nature of denizens that peopled Archibald Lawless's world by their sense of architecture and design. The room I entered was as beautiful and intense as young Lana Drexel. The ceilings were no less than eighteen feet high and the room was at least that in width—and more in length. The outer wall was one large pane of glass. There was no furniture in the room except for the wide, cushioned bench that ran from the front door to the picture window. Nine feet up on either side were large platforms that made for rooms without walls. Underneath the platform on the right everything was painted dark gray. The room formed underneath the platform on the left was white.

Miss Drexel threw herself down in the middle of the banquette. She was wearing a maroon kimono that barely came down to the tops of her thighs. This garment exposed shapely legs and powerful hamstrings. Her toenails were painted bright orange.

I sat down a few feet from her, near the window that looked south upon midtown.

"What does he want?" Lana said covering her eyes with an upturned hand.

"I don't really know," I said. "But he seems to think that you and Lansman and a few others are in trouble."

"Who?" She sat up and leaned toward me. The intensity of her stare was captivating and cold.

"Valerie Lox, Henry Lansman, Kenneth Cornell, Benny Lamarr, and you," I said. "Lamarr is also dead."

"How did he die?"

"A car accident I think. He was with a woman."

"What was her name?"

"I don't know."

The beauty lowered her face to her hands, causing her hair to fall forward. I could see her breasts under the mane of hair but somehow that didn't matter much.

"What does he want from me?" she asked.

"He wants to see you," I said.

She looked up at me again. "Will you protect me from him?"

"Yes," I said without hesitation. My heart went out to her and I think I might have even challenged A. Lawless for her smile.

12

We reached the Tessla building at about two in the afternoon. There were various business types coming in and out. The guard sitting in front of the Joan of Arc mural was an elderly white man with a big mustache and a head full of salt and pepper hair.

"Hello, Mr. Orlean," he hailed. "Mr. Lawless is expecting you and the lady."

"He is?"

"Yes sir."

The guard's eyes strayed over to Lana. She wore a Japanese ensemble of work pants and jacket made from rough cotton. The color was a drab green but still it accented her beauty.

"What's your name?" I asked the guard.

"Andy."

"I thought Lawless was in trouble with the building, Andy."

"No sir, Mr. Orlean. Why would you say that?"

"It was something about the rent."

"Oh," he said. Andy's smile was larger even than his mustache. "You mean the owners don't like him. Well, that might be true but you know the *men* in this building, the union men, they love Mr. Lawless. He's a legend in unions all over the city and the world. The reason they can't trick him outta here is that no real union man would ever turn a key on him."

In the elevator Lana stood close to me. When the doors slid open she squeezed my left forearm. I touched her hand. She kissed me lightly on the lips and smiled.

In the six seconds between the door opening and our departure she raised my blood pressure to a lethal level.

Archibald was waiting for us. He opened the door before I could knock and ushered us into chairs in the outer room.

I was later to learn that Lawless never had anyone but his closest confidants in his office.

"Miss Drexel," he said, smiling broadly.

Timidly, and leaning toward me on the hardback sofa, she said, "I hope that you'll be kind."

"I'll do you one better, lady," he said. "I'll be honest and I'll be fair."

She shivered.

I put a hand on her shoulder.

Archibald Lawless laughed.

"Let's get something straight from the start, Lana," he said. "Felix is working for me. He won't jump, lady, so straighten up and talk to me."

Lana did sit up. The woman who met me at the pink door returned. She was self-possessed and distant, a European princess being held for ransom in a Bedouin camp.

"What do you want?" she asked.

"Why did you come?" he replied.

"Because your employee told me that Hank Lansman and Benny Lamarr had been murdered."

Lawless smiled. I think he liked Lana.

"Why would that bother you?"

"Don't you know?"

He shook his head then shrugged his shoulders. "Someone in the government has gone to great lengths to hide the accidental deaths of your two friends. You got precious gems, hide away real estate, explosives, security, and a siren all mixed up together and then the hammer drops . . ."

Lana's eyes cut toward me for a moment then she turned them on the madman.

"What are you in this for?" she asked.

Walking the line, I said in my mind.

"I've been hired by the insurance company to locate some property that has been—temporarily misplaced," he said.

I was lost. Every step along the way he had presented himself as a dedicated anarchist, a man of the people. Now all of a sudden he was working for the Man.

Lana sat back. She seemed to relax.

"How much will they pay?" she asked.

"Five percent with a conviction," he said. "Eight if I can keep things quiet."

"Four million is a lot of revolution," she said. "But the full fifty could topple a nation."

"Are you worried about surviving or retiring?" Archibald asked the beauty.

It was her turn to smile enigmatically.

"Because you know," Lawless continued, "whoever it was killed Lansman and Lamarr will certainly come to your door one day soon."

"I'll die one day anyway," she admitted with a half pouting lower lip. "But to stay alive you have to keep on moving."

How old was she? I wondered. Four years and a century older than I.

"I ask you again," Lawless said. "Why did you come here?"

"No one says no to Mr. Archibald Lawless," she opined. "Just ask Andy downstairs."

"What do you want?" Lawless asked Lana.

"Hardly anything. Two hundred and fifty thousand will pay for my ticket out of town. And, of course, I expect exemption from arrest."

"Of course."

Lana stretched, looked at his murky eyes, and then nodded.

"Who were you working for?" he asked after an appreciative pause.

"Lamarr."

"To do what?"

"To go with him to a party in the Hamptons," she said sounding bored. "To meet a man named Strangman. To make friends with his bedroom."

"And did you?"

Her stare was her response.

"And then what?" Archibald asked.

"I met with Lansman, told him where the hidey hole was and collected my fee."

"That's all?"

"I met with the other people on your list," she admitted.

"When?"

"The morning after I spent with Strangman," she said. "He was really a jerk."

"Where did you meet?" Lawless asked.

"A vacant house that Val was selling. They wanted to go over the layout with me."

"And this Strangman," Lawless asked. "He was in the same business that Lamarr was in, I suppose?"

"I suppose," she replied.

"And was the operation a success?"

"I was paid."

"By who?" Lawless asked.

I wanted to correct his grammar but held my tongue.

"Lamarr." Lana hesitated. Her vast eyes were seeing something that had been forgotten.

"There was a guy with Lamarr," she said. "Normal looking. White. Forties."

"Was his hair short?" I asked.

"I think so."

"With a little gray?"

She turned to me, bit her lower lip, and then shook her head.

"I don't remember," she said. "He didn't make much of an impression. I thought that maybe he worked for Lamarr. Actually I'm pretty sure of it."

"So we have Stangman and a fortyish white man that might have worked for Lamarr," Lawless said.

"And Valerie Lox and Kenneth Cornell," I added.

The existentialist detective shook his head.

"No," he said. "Cornell made a mistake with a blasting cap yesterday afternoon and took off the top of his skull. Valerie Lox has disappeared. Maybe she's just smart but I wouldn't put a dollar on seeing her breathing again."

"What about me?" Lana Drexel asked.

"You're still breathing," he said.

"What should I do?"

"Nothing you've ever done before. Don't go home. Don't use your credit cards. Don't call anyone who has been on your phone bill in the last three years."

The young woman had a slight smile on her face as she listened to the anarchist's commandments.

"Do you have a suggestion of where I should go?" she asked.

"Sure. I'm full of advice. You just wait out here for a few minutes while I give my operative here his walking orders. Come on, Felix," he said to me. "Let's go in my office for a minute or two."

13

"She needs to be put somewhere very safe," Lawless told me, his profile set against the New Jersey landscape.

"Where?"

"There's a small chapel in Queens," he said. "Run by a defrocked priest I know."

"A friend of Red Tuesday's?"

He turned toward me and smiled. "That's why we're going to get along, kid," he said. "Because you know how to be funny."

"Do you want me to take her there?" I asked.

"No. If I let her spend more than an hour with you the next thing I know there you'd be face down with a knife in your back in some back alley in Cartegena."

His swampy eyes were laughing but I knew he believed what he said. *I* believed it. Inwardly I was relieved that I didn't have to accompany Lana Drexel to Queens.

"No," Lawless continued, "Lana can take care of herself and besides—I might have a little job for her."

"What kind of job?"

"The kind I wouldn't give you," he said.

"What should I do?"

"Follow the same plan I laid out for Miss Drexel. Don't do anything that you've done before."

"How can I not do anything I've done?" I asked. "I only have seven dollars on me. I don't know anything but my routine."

The anarchist smiled.

"Your first baby step outside the lies they have you living, young man."

"That doesn't help me."

"There's a hotel on East Thirty-fifth," he said. "Over by Park. It's called the Barony. Go there when you get tired. Tell Frederick that I told you to stay there tonight. Other than that you can do anything. Anything that you've never done before."

"Can I get an advance to eat with?"

"Frederick will feed you."

"What if want to go to a movie?"

Lawless shook his head. I could see his thoughts: *Here the child could do anything and all he can come up with is a movie.*

"Or maybe opera tickets," I added.

"I never carry more than ten dollars in cash myself," he said.

"But I don't have a credit card."

"Neither do I." He held his pious palms upward.

"How do you make it with only ten bucks in your pocket?"

"It's a challenge," he said. "And challenge is what makes life sing."

I must have looked miserable because he gave me his quick laugh and said, "In your office. The bottom half of the pink file. Eighteen, eighteen, nine."

With that he rose and went to the door.

"When do I see you again?" I asked.

"I'll call you," he said. "Be prepared."

With that he left the office. I heard him say a few words to Lana Drexel. She laughed and said something. And then they were gone.

I felt uncomfortable staying in his private office. It seemed so personal in there. There were private letters on his closed laptop and all those curiosities along the walls. I went to the storage room, what he called my office, and sat at the long table in a chair that seemed to be made from stoneware pottery clay. It was glazed a shiny dark red and slender in every aspect. I wouldn't have been surprised if it broke under the weight of a man Lawless's size.

I perused a couple of Red Tuesday's newsletters. The paranoia struck a note with me though and so I put them down.

I wondered about what Lawless had said; that we lived in a skein of lies. So many things he said seemed to be anchored in some greater truth. In many ways he was like my father, certain and powerful—with all of the answers, it seemed.

But Lawless was wild. He took chances and had received some hard knocks. He lived with severe mental illness and shrugged off threats that would turn brave men into jellyfish.

Don't do anything you've done before, he told me. I experienced the memory of his words like a gift.

I picked up the phone and entered a number from a slip of paper in my pocket.

"Hello?" she answered. "Who is this?"

There was a lot of noise in the background, people talking and the clatter of activity.

"Felix."

"Who?"

"The guy you gave your number yesterday at lunch . . . I had the soba noodles."

"Oh. Hi."

"I was wondering if you wanted to get together tonight. After work I mean."

"Oh. I don't know. I was going to go with some of the guys here to . . . But I don't have to. What did you want to do?"

"I'm pretty open," I said. "Anything you been really wanting to do?"

"Well," she hesitated.

"What?"

"There's a chamber music concert up at the Cloisters tonight. It's supposed to be wonderful up there."

"That sounds great," I said, really meaning it.

"But the tickets are seventy-five dollars . . . each."

"Hold on," I said.

I stretched the phone cord over to the tiny pink file cabinet. The drawers were facing the wall so I turned it around—it was much heavier than I expected.

I could see that the bottom drawer was actually a safe with a combination lock.

"Are you still there?" Sharee said.

"Oh yeah. Listen, Sharee . . ."

"What?"

"Can I call you right back?"

"Okay."

It took me a moment to recall the numbers eighteen eighteen nine. The combination worked the first time.

There was more cash in that small compartment than I had ever seen. Stacks of hundred-dollar bills and fifties and twenties. English pounds and piles of euros. There were pesos and other bills in white envelopes that were from other, more exotic parts of the world.

"Wow."

I took two hundred and fifty dollars leaving an IOU in its place. Then I hit the redial button.

"Felix?" she answered.

"What time do you get off work?"

Sharee was a music student at Julliard. She studied oboe and flute. There was an oboe in the quartet and a violin that made my heart thrill. After the concert we walked along the dark roads of the Cloisters' park. I kissed her against a moss covered stone wall and she ran her hands up under my sweater scratching her long fingernails across my shoulder blades.

We took a taxi down to the Barony. At first the desk clerk didn't want to get Frederick but when I mentioned Mr. Lawless he jumped to the task.

Frederick was a tall man, white from his hair to his shoes. He guided us to a small elevator and brought us to a room that was small and lovely. It was red and purple and mostly bed.

I must have kissed Sharee's neck for over an hour before trying to remove her muslin blouse. She pulled the waistband of her skirt up over her belly and said, "Don't look at me. I'm fat."

That's when I started kissing around her belly button. It was an inny and very deep. Every time I pressed my tongue down there she gasped and dug her nails into my shoulders.

"What are you doing to me?" she said.

"Didn't anybody ever kiss you here before?" I asked her. "It's just so sexy." And then I jammed my tongue down deep.

We spent the night finding new places on each other. It was almost a game and we were almost children. We didn't even go to the bathroom alone.

At five I ordered room service. Salami sandwiches and coffee.

"Who are you, Felix Orlean?" she asked me as we stared at each other over the low coffee table that held our early morning meal.

"Just a journalism student," I said. "In over my head every way that I look."

She was wearing my sweater and nothing else. I wanted to kiss her belly but she looked too comfortable to unfold out of that chair.

"I have a kinda boyfriend," she said.

"Huh?"

"Are you mad?"

"How could I be mad?" I said. "What you gave me last night was exactly what I needed. And you're so beautiful."

"But I'm not very nice," she said, experimenting with the thought of being beautiful while at the same time feeling guilty about her deceit.

"I think you are."

"But here I am smelling like you in your sweater and he's in the East Village sleeping in his bed."

"And here you are and here I am," I said. "Everybody's got to be someplace."

She came over and began kissing my navel then.

The phone rang. It was the last thing in the world that I wanted but I knew that I had to answer.

Sharee moaned in distress.

"Just a minute, honey," I said. "It might be business. Hello?"

"Between Sixth and Seventh on the north side of Forty-seventh Street," Archibald Lawless said. "Deluxe Jewelers. Nine thirty. I'll meet you out front."

The moment I hung up the phone Sharee whispered in my ear, "Give me three days and I'm yours."

I grunted and pulled her blue-streaked hair so that her lips met mine. And for a long time I didn't think about big-eyed models or anarchy or where the day might end.

14

I was standing across the street from the jewelry store at nine fifteen, sipping coffee from a paper cup and rubbing the sand from my eyes. When I say jewelry store I should be more specific. That block is all jewelers. Almost every doorway and almost every floor. There were Arabs and India Indians and Orthodox Jews, white men and Asian men and every other race counted on that block. Big black security guards joked with small wizened dealers. I heard French and Spanish, Hebrew and Yiddish, Chinese and even a Scandinavian tongue casually spoken by passersby.

I had put Sharee in a taxi an hour before. She said that she was going to get some sleep and that I should call her later that day. I told her that I'd call that day if I could and she asked if I was in trouble.

"Why you say that?"

"My daddy was always in trouble and you remind me of him."

"I like it when you call me daddy," I said before kissing her and closing the yellow cab door.

Deluxe Jewelers was just a glass door with unobtrusive gold letters telling of its name. There was an older brown man, with an almond shaped head accented by a receding hairline, sitting on a fold-up metal chair inside the door. There were many more impressive stores on that block. Stores with display cases lined with precious stones set in platinum and gold.

I figured that the people who worked at Deluxe were Lawless's low-rent toehold in this world of unending wealth.

"Hey, kid," Archibald Lawless said.

He was standing there next to me as if he had appeared out of thin air.

"Mr. Lawless."

"Being on time is a virtue in this world," he said. I wasn't sure if that was a compliment or an indictment. "Shall we?"

We crossed the street and went through the modest entrance.

"Mr. Lawless," the seated guard hailed. "You here for Sammy?"

"I think I need Applebaum today, Larry."

The sentry nodded and said, "Go on then."

The room he sat in was no more than a vestibule. There was a black tiled floor, his chair, and an elevator door. Lawless pressed the one button on the panel and the door opened immediately. On the panel inside there were twelve buttons, in no particular order, marked only by colors. The anarchist chose orange and the car began to descend.

When the door opened we entered into another small and nondescript room. It was larger than Larry's vestibule but with no furniture and a concrete floor.

There was a closed door before us.

This opened and a small Asian woman came out. Her face was as hard as a Brazil nut until she saw Lawless. She smiled and released a stream of some Asian dialect. Archibald answered in the same language, somewhat slower but fluent still and all.

We followed the woman down a hall of open doorways, each one leading to rooms with men and women working on some aspect of gemstones. In one room there was an elderly Jewish man looking down on a black velvet-lined board. On the dark material lay at least a dozen diamonds, every one large enough to choke a small bird.

At the end of the hall was a doorless doorway through which I could see a dowdy office and an unlikely man.

He stood up to meet us but wasn't much taller than am I. He was brown with blond hair and striking emerald green eyes. He was both hideous and beautiful, qualities that don't come together well in men.

"Archie," he said in an accent I couldn't place. "It's been so long."

They shook hands.

"Vin, this is Felix. He's working for me," Lawless said.

"So happy to meet you." The jeweler took my hand and gazed into my eyes.

I suppressed a shudder and said, "Me too."

There were chairs and so we sat. Vin Applebaum went behind his battered oak desk. We were underground and so there were no windows. The office, which wasn't small, had been painted so long ago that it was a toss-up what color it had been originally. The lighting was fluorescent and the Persian carpet was threadbare where it had been regularly traversed.

Applebaum, who was somewhat over forty, wore an iridescent silver and green suit. It was well tailored with three buttons. His shirt was black and open at the throat.

The most surprising thing to me about his dress was that he wore no jewelry. No ring or chain or even a watch. He was like a gay male pimp who specialized in women or a vegan butcher.

"Strangman," Lawless said.

"Lionel," Vin replied.

"If you say so. What about him?"

"He was the luckiest man in the world there for a while. Through an investment syndicate he made a purchase that kings salivate over. Now he's in bad trouble. As bad as it can be."

"He was robbed?"

"That word doesn't begin to explain the loss of twenty-three nearly red diamonds."

"Red?" Lawless said. "I thought the most you could get in a diamond was pink or purple."

Applebaum nodded. "Yes. You might say that these stones, not one of which is less than six karats, are a deep or dark pink. But to the eye beholding they are red."

"Fifty million dollars red?"

"If you could sell the whole collection," Applebaum said, nodding. "Yes. Think of the necklace you could make with just nine of those gems."

"My scales run to starving, dying millions," Lawless said.

"You could feed a small country with Strangman's find."

"What about Lamarr?" Archibald Lawless asked then.

I wondered if he were really working for an insurance company. I realized that even if he had a client that their needs might dovetail like the interests of a gem dealer and a mad anarchist in a basement room in Manhattan.

"Benny?" Applebaum asked. "What about him?"

"Did he know Strangman?"

"Everyone knows Lionel. He's been on the periphery of our business for many years. Do you think that Benny had anything to do with the theft?"

"The diamonds were definitely stolen then?" Lawless asked.

"Definitely."

"Who has them?"

Applebaum shook his head.

"Who insured them then?" Lawless asked.

"Auchschlous, Anterbe, and Grenell. An Australian company." Again the odd jeweler shook his head.

"What's wrong with them?"

"Strangman is old-fashioned. He likes to carry stones around in his pocket," the ugly diamond dealer said. "A lot of the old-timers are like that. Somebody says that all they would need is fifty thousand dollars and life would even out and Strangman would pull two hundred thousand in diamonds out of his vest pocket just to show them how small they really are. Stupid."

"The insurance didn't cover personal delivery?" I asked just to feel that I wouldn't blend in with the colorless walls.

"That's right," Applebaum said with a generous smile. "Somebody made a deal with Strangman. A deal so sweet and so secure that he brought the stones home and made an appointment with the buyer."

Archibald Lawless's eyes were closed. His hands were held upward. He began nodding his head as if he were listening to a subtle tune coming from a bit too far off.

"Who is the investigating agent?" he asked behind still closed eyes.

"Jules Vialet," Applebaum said without hesitation.

The anarchist opened his eyes and asked, "How did you know that so quickly?"

"Because he's AAG's best man and even though they have a clause saying that he couldn't carry the jewels without proper protection he still might be able to make a case against them."

"And what about Strangman," Lawless asked. "Is he still around?"

"Up at Obermann's Sanitarium on sixty-eighth."

"He's fakin' it?"

"I doubt it," Vin said. "He never had much money or much power. Those stones represented a whole new life for him on these streets. All he needed was that collection in his vault and he would have had the respect of the whole community. Now, of course, all of that is gone."

There was great deal of pleasure Applebaum felt about the professional demise of Lionel Strangman. I got the feeling that life in the jewelry district wasn't friendly or safe.

15

There was a silver-gray Cadillac waiting for us when we came out. A dark man with broad shoulders, and a neck an inch too short, climbed out of the driver's seat to greet us.

"Mr. Lawless," he said in a Caribbean-English accent. "Where do you wish to go, sir?"

"This is Felix Orlean," Lawless said. "Felix, meet Derek Chambers."

The chauffeur's hands were rough and strong. He was shorter than Lawless, only about six feet.

"Pleased to meet you, Derek," I said.

"We're going to an address somewhere in Manhattan," Lawless said. "I'll need the phone books."

Derek opened the back door and Lawless slipped in, moving all the way to the other side in order to make room for me. I got in and the door shut behind me. The chauffeur went to the rear of the car, opened the trunk and closed it. After he'd climbed into the driver's seat he handed my temporary employer the white book and Yellow Pages for New York City.

Derek drove off and Lawless began thumbing through the Yellow Pages, the business to business volume.

"Corruption on this level is always pretty easy to crack," he was saying. "Big companies, rich men, and the government are all too arrogant to waste time hiding their crimes. They have official avenues to follow and reports to make, agents with health benefits and paramours who nurse aspirations of their own.

"Derek, take us to Second Avenue between Fifty-fourth and Fifty-fifth."

"Yes sir, Mister Lawless."

"Is that your real name?" I asked. "Lawless?"

The nihilist smiled at me and patted my knee.

"You would even question a man's name?" he asked, amazed.

"I mean what are the odds?" I said. "An anarchist named Lawless? That's just too perfect."

"What if my parents were revolutionists? What if I looked up my name and decided that that's what I'd become?"

"Your parents were revolutionaries that changed their names?" I asked.

"I am Archibald Lawless," he said. "I'm sitting here before you. You are looking into my eyes and questioning what you see and what you hear. On the streets you meet Asian men named Brian, Africans named Joe Cramm. But you don't questions their obviously being named for foreign devils. You accept their humiliation. You accept their loss of history. You accept them being severed from long lines of heritage by their names. Why wouldn't you accept just as simply my liberating appellation?"

"I . . ." I said.

"Here we are," Derek announced.

The building must have been considered futuristic and quirky when it was newly built. It still had a personality, if somewhat cold. Gray steel and stone relieved by thick glass windows that were accented by just a touch of green tinting. Two guards sat at a violet kidney-shaped desk with computer screens embedded in the top.

"Yes?" the smaller one asked me.

"Lawless," I said. "Archibald and associate for Mr. Vialet."

There were lights on in the entranceway but darkness hovered at the corners of the room. That gloom ascended to the roof.

The guard flipped through a screen, found a number and then dialed it on an old-fashioned rotary phone.

"A man named Lawless and somebody else for Mr. Vialet," the guard said.

He listened for a beat or two and then said to us, "Please have a seat. Someone'll be down to get you."

There was a whole tree that had been split down the middle and then cut to the length of a twelve-foot bench for us to sit on. The tree-half had been heavily lacquered and fitted with dowels to keep it from rolling around when someone sat on it.

"They rule the world," Archibald Lawless hissed.

He was sitting next to me with his hands on his knees. He still wore black slacks and an army jacket buttoned half the way up his chest. Now that his jacket was open I noticed that he wore a necklace too. It was strung with chicken bones that were white from age and being exposed to the sun. The bones had a crazy clattery way about them. There wasn't much doubt why the security guard decided to ask me about our business.

"Who?" I asked.

"People in buildings like this one. They own farms in Turkey and solar generation plants in the Gobi desert. They decide on foreign legislation and cry over the deaths of their children. Even their love is hypocritical. Even with their deaths they cannot pay for their crimes . . ."

He would have said more but a young man in a lavender suit approached us.

"Mr. Lawless?" he asked me.

"No," I said.

The kid was pale and definitely an ectomorph. But he'd been doing his exercises. There was muscle under his lapels and on his toothpick shoulders. In his eyes however he was still a ninety-pound weakling. He stared at Lawless as if the big man were a plains lion hungry for a pale-boy snack.

"You're Lawless?"

"Mr. Archibald Lawless."

"Yes," the young man said. "I'm Grant Harley, Mr. Vialet's assistant. Please follow me."

He led us through a hallway that had as a path a raised ramp that went over a hall-long pond filled with oversized, multicolored carp. Bamboo sprouted from planters along the sides of the walls. We entered into a large room inhabited by five secretaries, each at her own pastel colored desk. The were windows in this room and classical flute playing instead of Muzak.

One of the secretaries, a forty-year-old black woman with a broad chest and small eyes, got up and approached us.

"You Lawless?" she asked me.

"I'm Mr. Lawless," Archibald said.

The woman didn't seem to like his sense of self-worth but I think she was more intimidated by his size and growl.

"This way," she said.

We went through a smallish doorway into a long dark hall. At the end of this hall was a white door. The secretary opened the door and brought us into a large room with a sunken office at its center. We had to walk down five stairs to get on an even plane with the desk behind which sat a man who was almost indescribable he was so plain.

He stood to his five foot nine height and looked at us with bland brown eyes. His hair was brown and his skin was off-white. His hands were as normal as you could be. The suit he wore was medium gray and the shirt might have had a few blue threads in the depths of all that white.

"Archibald," he said to the right man.

"Do I know you?" my would-be employer asked.

"No. But I sure know a lot about you. There was an emerald necklace that we lost in Sri Lanka six years ago that no one ever thought we'd recover. One day you just walked in and dropped it off. Gave the fee to some charity as I remember."

"Can we sit down, Mr. Vialet?"

"Certainly. Forgive me. What is your friend's name?"

"Felix," I said. "Orlean."

"Have a seat, Felix, Archibald. Right here on the sofa."

It was a fuzzy white sofa that sat across from his desk. There was a dark stained walnut coffee table before us. Vialet sat in a plain walnut chair.

"Anything to drink?" he offered.

"Lets talk about red diamonds," Lawless replied.

"I like a man who gets down to business," Jules Vialet said. "Business is what makes the world turn."

". . . like a stone over the bones of the innocent," Lawless added. "Who do you suspect in the theft?"

"I'm really not at liberty to discuss the disposition of any active case that we are pursuing, Mr. Lawless. But if—"

Archibald stood up.

"Come on, Felix," he said.

Before I could rise the insurance investigator was on his feet, holding up both hands.

"Don't be like that," he said. "You know there are rules that I have to follow."

"I don't have time for your rules, Mr. Insurance Man. People have been dying out there and your government is covering it up. There's something rotten in this business and I'm the one's going to sanitize and bleach it clean."

"What do you mean about the government?" Vialet asked.

"You answer me, Mr. Insurance Man, and then I'll share."

"That's hardly fair, you know," Vialet said. "What if I give you all my information and then you turn around and leave or tell me that you really don't know anything?"

"I'm not the liar here," Lawless said. "You are. This whole building is a lie. Your pale-faced boy and your snotty secretaries are lies. Maybe if you ate raw flesh at your desk and kept a pot of shit at each doorway then maybe you'd be halfway to the truth about something. No. I'm not a liar, Mr. Insurance Man. I'm the only true thing you've seen all year."

His voice sounded a little high, strained. I worried that maybe one of his psychological maladies was manifesting itself.

"Mr. Lawless," I said.

When he turned toward me I could see the madness in his eyes. "What?"

"We don't have the briefcase with us so I won't be able to make complete notes."

For a moment he was bewildered but then his mind grabbed hold. He laughed and said, "It's okay, Felix. We'll just wing it until we have the case." He looked back at Vialet and said, "Tell me, who do you suspect in the theft?"

Vialet looked at us and sighed. He sat down and so did Lawless.

"A man named Lamarr," the insurance man said.

"Benny," Lawless agreed. "Him and Lana Drexel. And Valerie Lox, Kenneth Cornell, and Henry Lansman. We know the soldiers. What we want is the bankroll."

I could see that Vialet was concentrating on the names Lawless threw out.

"You seem to know more than I do," he said.

"Who is the man who has been traveling with Lamarr lately?" Archibald asked. "A white man in his forties. He has short hair, maybe graying, maybe not."

"Wayne Sacorliss," Vialet said without hesitation. "He's been around Lamarr for a few years. Just as toady as far as we can tell. He has an office on Lexington, just south of Forty-first."

"Who's the buyer?" Lawless asked.

"We think it's a Canadian name Rudolph Bickell. He's a very rich man and a collector of rare gems. He lives in Las Vegas half the year."

"How does he make his money?"

"Buying and selling," Vialet said. "Your grain to bakeries, cotton to sweatshops in Asia, metal to gun makers and guns to the highest bidder."

"Weapons?"

"Anything," Vialet said. "He'd been making noise to Strangman about buying the gemstones until about three months ago. We figure that when he came up with the plan he stopped calling."

"How much?" Lawless asked.

"We'll go as high as three million. That's all the stones in perfect condition. No trouble to cover either."

"Will corroboration by the police about my central role in re-claiming the jewels be enough?" Lawless asked in flawless business contract style.

"Certainly," Vialet allowed.

"Come on, Felix," Archibald said.

We were out of the gray insurance building in less than five minutes.

16

"I thought that you were an anarchist," I was saying, "a political purist, a man of the people."

Lawless was sitting next to me in the back seat of Derek Chambers's limo, scanning the white pages.

"That sounds right to me," he said. "But mostly, Felix, like I told you before, I walk that line."

"So the three million means nothing to you?"

"That money will pay for a lot of walking, son. Slaves walking across borders, bound men dancing again—that's what it'll pay for, and more."

He gave Derek an address on Lexington.

Sacorliss ran an optical glass frame distribution business on the fourteenth floor. Many of the offices around him were empty. The reception room had been uninhabited for some while. There was dust on the blotter and no evidence that the phone was even plugged in. I wondered if Wayne Sacorliss had moved on to LensCrafters or some other larger optical business.

"Hello," I called.

There was a doorway beyond the reception desk leading to a passageway formed from opaque glass panels. This hallway was in the form of an L that one would suspect led to the main office.

"Who's there?" a mild mannered male voice inquired.

"Archibald Lawless," I said, "and his assistant." I couldn't get my tongue around the word scribe.

A man appeared in the glass angle. From the front he could have been the man I saw running from the death of Henry Lansman. Only this man wore a light brown suit instead of a red parka.

"Who?" he asked.

"We've come to ask you about Benny Lamarr," Lawless said.

Sacorliss had light blue eyes and a broad face. His eyes were elliptical in both shape and manner. His lips were so sensual they belonged on a younger man, or a slightly perverse demigod. His features were all that he showed. There wasn't even a glimmer of recognition for the man he assisted.

He didn't respond at all.

"Can we go into your office, Mr. Sacorliss?" I asked.

"Are you here to buy frames?"

"No."

"Then I don't see what we have to talk about."

"Henry Lansman for one thing," I said.

From the corner of my eye I saw Lawless swivel his head to regard me.

"I don't know who that is," Sacorliss was saying, "but if you must come in then follow me."

At the end of the L-shaped glass hall was a round room lined on one side by waist-high, old fashioned windows that were furbished with brown tinted glass. I could see people in offices not twenty feet away. Some were working and others talking. It was a pleasant proletariat view of the inner workings of a big city's commerce.

This room was also quite desolate. One maple desk with a square-cut oak chair, a telephone with a bare cord that ran across the room to find the jack in the opposite wall. There was a laptop computer on the floor and not one scrap of paper anywhere.

Sacorliss was a few inches taller than I and maybe twenty pounds more than he should have been. But he moved with grace and self-confidence. Once we were in the room he closed the door.

Lawless's eyes never left the smaller man. His wariness made me nervous but I didn't know what to do. So I perched myself on the edge of the maple desk while Wayne Sacorliss and Archibald faced each other.

"What is it you want from me?" Sacorliss asked the amber king before him.

"There's no need for trouble here, Wayne. I'm just interested in why the government wants to cover up Lansman's death, his and a few others whom you might or might not know."

Lawless's mouth turned up in a smile but his eyes were dull.

The baby finger of his left hand twitched.

Sacorliss moved a few inches to his right so that his back was turned fully toward me. Seeing his head from this position I was sure that he was the same man I saw fleeing the scene of Henry Lansman's death. I wanted to signal Lawless that we had what we needed but all of his attention was on the killer.

"I furnish frames for optical lenses, Mr. um, Lawless, wasn't it?"

"There's no need for conflict between us, Wayne," Lawless said in a uncharacteristically placating tone. "Felix here and I just want to know about who would want to hide the murders of international criminals. Especially when those murders were so well executed that no doctor would suspect foul play."

What happened next took me a few days to work out. Sacorliss lifted his right shoulder in a way that made me think he was about to deny any knowledge of Lawless's insinuations. Then Archibald took half a step backwards. Sacorliss moved the same distance forward by taking a step with his left foot. Then the assassin shouted and I felt a powerful impact against my chest. I flew backward over the desk, hit the floor and slid into the wall.

While I was still en route to the wall Sacorliss produced a very slender ten-inch blade from somewhere in his suit. He lunged at his anarchist inquisitor and stabbed him in the chest.

Lawless wasn't slow, however. He grabbed Sacorliss's arm at the elbow so that the tip of the blade went less than half an inch into his body.

I struggled to my feet coughing hard. The vision I saw was surreal: Before me the two men were struggling like the titans in Goya's black painting. Sacorliss's knife was still piercing Lawless's chest but the larger man was managing to impede the progress of the blade. Through the window two women were talking, a whole office full of workers were walking back and forth, there was even a man looking up from his keyboard staring dreamily toward the battle.

Sacorliss kicked Lawless in the thigh with a quick movement. He did this twice more and I knew that sooner or later the man I came in with would be dead. I tried the door but it was locked. I was still coughing and stunned from the roundhouse kick the killer had hit me with. I looked for something to hit him with. I tried to lift his oak chair but it was too heavy to get up over my head.

I was about to go for the laptop when Sacorliss tried another kick. Lawless moved his thigh and the assassin lost his balance. Lawless then lifted him up over his head. That's when the most amazing thing happened. Somehow Archibald managed to disarm Sacorliss so that when he slammed him down on the floor he also stabbed him through the chest.

Sacorliss kicked Lawless away and jumped to his feet. He looked at me and then at the computer. He took a step toward the laptop but his foot betrayed him and he went down on one knee. He looked at his killer then.

"Who are you?" I heard him ask. And then he fell face forward and I think he was dead.

Blood seeped toward the laptop.

Lawless turned Sacorliss over with a toe.

"Get the computer," he said to me.

While I did that, he wiped the haft of the knife clean of fingerprints.

People were still gabbing and working in the office building across the way.

On the way out, Lawless made sure that the doorknob was clean of prints. By the time we were back in Derek's limo, I was so cold that my teeth were chattering. Soon after that I lost consciousness.

17

When I woke up it was dark. I was still dressed and on my back on a bed that was fully made. There was a scented candle burning and mild recorder music wafting in from somewhere. I felt odd, both peaceful and numb. My hands were lying at my sides and I felt no need to move them. I remembered the death of Wayne Sacorliss and the bizarre witnesses from the windows across the way. I thought about the blood across the barren wood floor but none of that bothered me. I supposed that Lawless had given me some kind of sedative from his medical case; something to relax my nerves. I was grateful for whatever he'd done because I knew that unaided I would have been in the depths of anxious despair.

A feathery touch skimmed my brow. I turned to see a woman, somewhere near fifty but still very attractive, sitting at my side.

"You had quite a scare," she said.

"Where am I?"

"Have you ever been to Queens?" she asked with a smile.

"Kennedy Airport."

She was slight and pale with crystalline blue eyes and long fingers. She wore a cream colored dress. The bodice was raw silk and the rest was made from the more refined version of that material. It seemed as if her hair were platinum blonde instead of white.

"Who are you?" I asked.

"A friend of Archibald," she said. "He's downstairs now. Would you like to see him?"

"I don't know if I can get up."

"Once you start moving it wears off," she said.

She took my hand and stood up, pulling me. She had no strength but I followed her lead. I worried that when I got to my feet I'd be dizzy but I wasn't. As a matter of fact I felt very good.

Outside the bedroom was a short hallway that shared space with a staircase leading down. Everything was covered in thick green carpeting and so our footsteps were silent.

On the first floor was a sitting room with two sofas and three stuffed chairs. Archibald Lawless, wearing a gold colored two-piece suit and a ochre shirt was sitting in one of the chairs with his feet up on a small stool.

"Felix. How are you, son?"

"You killed that man."

"I certainly did. Maybe if you hadn't told him about Lansman I could have kept him alive but—"

"You mean you blame you killing him on me?"

"As soon as you mentioned Lansman he was sure that we had identified him as the assassin. It was either us or him. I tried to tell him that I didn't care but he was a professional and he had to at least try and kill us."

I sat down on the corner of a sofa nearest to him.

"How can you be so cavalier about a murder?" I asked.

"I did not murder him," he replied. "I saved our lives. That man was a stone cold killer. If I hadn't been keeping up with my tai chi he would have gutted me and then cut your throat."

I remembered the impact of his kick against my chest and the speed with which he attacked the seemingly unassailable Lawless.

"What about all those witnesses?"

"There were no witnesses."

"The people in the windows across the way. We were in plain sight of them."

"Oh no," Lawless said, shaking his spiky head. "Those windows were one-way panes. I've used the same brand myself."

"So no one saw?"

"No. And even if they did. He was trying to kill us. That was self-defense, Felix."

"Would either of you boys like to have some tea?" our hostess asked.

"I'd like some English Breakfast if you have it, ma'am," I said.

She smiled at me and said, "I like this one, Arch. You should hold onto him."

"He doesn't want to work for me, Red. Thinks that it's too dangerous."

She smiled again. "Green tea for you?"

Lawless nodded and she made her way out of the room.

"What did you call her?" I asked.

"Red."

"Red Tuesday?"

"Has she asked you if you were Catholic yet?"

For some reason I hadn't thought that Red Tuesday was a real person. At least not a beautiful middle-aged woman living in a standard working class home.

"If she does," Lawless continued, "Tell her that your parents are but that you have lapsed in your faith."

"Okay."

"Now," he said. "Lets talk about what we have to do tonight."

"Tonight? I'm not doing anything with you tonight or any other time. You killed that man."

"Did I have a choice?"

"*I* have a choice," I said. "The choice not to be in the same room with you."

"Yes," he said, nodding at me. "But this is a deep problem, Felix. You can see that even I'm in danger here. Sacorliss was an assassin. We certainly ran the danger of a violent confrontation with such a man. But now we're going to a sanitarium, to see a sick man. There's no danger involved."

"Why the hell do you need me in the first place?" I said. "You never even knew me before three days ago. How can I possibly help someone like you?"

"My kind of work is lonely, Felix. And maybe it's a little bit crazy. I've spent a whole lifetime trying to fix broken systems, making sure that justice is served. Lately I've been lagging a little. Slowing down, breaking down, making mistakes that could be fatal. Having you by me has given me a little bit of an edge, some confidence that I hadn't even known was eroded.

"All I ask is that you stick with me until we find the answer to why Sacorliss was activated. Just stick with me until the police believe they have the killer of Henry Lansman."

"I thought he had a heart attack?"

"No. He was accosted by an aerosol toxin. The autopsy showed that last night. And there's a warrant out for your arrest in connection with that killing."

"Me?"

"English Breakfast," Red Tuesday said as she came into the room. "And green tea for man who watches his health and the health of the enslaved world."

She carried the delicate teacups on a silver tray, proffering us our drinks.

"Felix?" she said.

"Yes, Ms. Tuesday?"

"Are you a Catholic by any chance?"

"My parents are, ma'am, but I never went after I was twelve."

Oberman's Sanitarium had only a small brass sign on the wall to identify itself. Otherwise you would have thought it was a residential prewar building like all its neighbors on the block.

It was twelve-fifteen by the time Derek dropped us off.

Lawless rang the bell and stood there in his gold suit, carrying his medical briefcase. He looked like a rattlesnake in a Sunday bonnet, a stick of dynamite with chocolate coating up to the fuse.

I was sickened by events of the day but still I knew I had to stay with the anarchist because that was the only way for me to keep on top of what was happening. If I left then, even if I ran and went back to New Orleans, I would be vulnerable to dangerous people who could get at me without me ever knowing they were near. And there would still be a warrant out for my arrest.

The door was opened by a woman wearing all white. She was young, tall, and manlike in her demeanor and visage.

"Lawless?" she asked me.

"It's him," I said.

"Come quickly."

We hustled into the building.

She led us to an elevator made for two and took us to the sixth floor.

When we got out she said, "Do you have it?"

Lawless took out a large wallet from his front pocket and counted out five one-hundred-dollar bills. He handed these to the manly nurse.

"No funny stuff," she said as she folded the bills into her white apron.

"What room is he in?" Lawless responded.

"Seven."

18

I was surprised by the hominess of the room. Darkish yellow walls with a real wood-framed bed and knickknacks on the shelves and bureaus. On the wall with the largest expanse hung a framed picture that was at least six feet wide and almost that in height. The colors were buff and pale blue. It was a beach at first light. Almost devoid of details it seemed to me a commentary on the beginning of the world.

In a small padded chair next to the one window a thin white man sat looking out on the street. He wore a gray robe over striped blue and white pajamas. His elbows were on his knees, his small mustache was crooked.

"I, I, I thought you were here for me," he said softly.

The only clue that we were in some kind of medical facility was metal tray-table at the foot of the bed. There was a medical form on a clipboard hanging from the side. Lawless unhooked the clipboard and began to read.

"Yes," he said to the patient. "I was told that you're suffering from a mild breakdown. I was called by Dr. Samson to administer Cronomicin."

"Wh-what's that?"

Lawless put his briefcase on the metal table and opened it. He took out a hypodermic needle that had already been filled with a pinkish fluid.

Gesturing at the needle, he said, "This will alleviate your anxiety and impose a feeling of calm that will allow you to sleep and wake up without a care in the world."

I wondered if he had given me some of the same juice.

"Why haven't they, why haven't they given it to me before?" Lionel Strangman asked.

"Cronomicin is very expensive. There was a hang-up with the insurance." Lawless's smile was almost benign.

"You don't look like a doctor." Strangman seemed to be speaking to someone behind the big amber liar.

"Catch me at office hours and I'll have on my smock just like everybody else."

"Maybe I should—" Strangman started.

"Give me your arm," Lawless commanded.

The thin white man did as he was told.

Lawless took a cotton swab and alcohol from his briefcase, cleaned a spot on Strangman's arm, and then began to search for a vein. I turned my back on them. I don't know why exactly. Maybe I thought if I didn't see the injection I couldn't bear witness in court.

I went to the picture on the wall. It wasn't a print, as I had at first thought, but an original oil painting. It was old too. From a few feet distant the beige sky and faint water looked to be seamless. But up close I could make out thousands of small brushstrokes composed of dozens of colors. I imagined some asylum patient of another century making this painting for the inmates of today.

"How are you feeling, Mr. Strangman?" Archibald Lawless was asking the man in the chair.

"Good," he said without hesitation. "Peaceful. Maybe I should lie down."

"In a minute. First I'd like to ask you a few questions."

"Okay."

"Dr. Samson told me that you had the collapse after a theft."

"Yes," he said. He looked down at his hands. "Funny, it doesn't seem so important now. They were beautiful, you know. Almost like rubies."

"They were stolen from a safe in your home?" Dr. Lawless asked.

"Yes." Strangman looked up. His eyes were beatific as if they were meant to be paired with that painting of the primordial first day. "I woke up and they were gone. They must have drugged me because the police said that they used an explosive on the safe."

He brought hands to lips as a reflex of grief but the sorrow was forgotten now with Lawless's elixir in his veins.

"Do you know Benny Lamarr?" Lawless asked.

"Why yes. How did you know that?"

"He called to ask how you were doing. Him and his friend Wayne Sacorliss."

"Wayne. To look at him you'd never think that he was from Lebanon, would you?"

"No," Lawless said carelessly. "It surprised me that he was a Moslem."

"Oh no," Strangman said in high feminine voice. "Christian. Christian. His mother was from Armenia. But he's an American now."

"Did you work with him?"

"No. He works for Benny. Poor Benny."

"Why do you say that?" Lawless asked.

"He brought his fiancée to a party at my house. The next night she was in my bed." Even under the spell of the narcotic Strangman was a dog.

"Who are you?" I asked Archibald Lawless.

We were sitting in the window seat of a twenty-four-hour diner on the West Side Highway at 2:57 A.M.

"You're not questioning my name again, are you?"

"No. Not that. How did you get into that clinic? How did you know what drug to give Strangman? How did you know what that killer was thinking? No one man can do all these things."

"You're right."

"I thought so. Who do you work for? Really."

"You're a very intelligent young man, Felix. But intelligence alone doesn't help you rise above. You see clearly, more clearly, than most, but you don't apprehend.

"I am, everyone is, a potential sovereignty, a nation upon my own. I am responsible for every action taken in my name and for every step that I take—or that I don't take. When you get to the place that you can see yourself as a completely autonomous, self-governing entity then everything will come to you; everything that you will need."

A waiter brought us coffee then. I sat there drinking, thinking about the past few days. I had missed two seminars and a meeting with my advisor. I hadn't been home, though I doubted if my room-mate would notice. I had been arrested for suspicion of my involvement in a murder, made love to by a woman I didn't really know, I had been an accessory to a killing, and party to the illegal impersonation of a doctor—in addition to the unlawful administration of contraband drugs. I was temporarily in the employ of a madman and involved in the investigation of the theft of millions of dollars in diamonds. And, even though I was aware of all those aspects of the past few days, I was still almost totally in the dark.

"What are we doing, Mr. Lawless? What are we involved in?"

He smiled at me. The swamp of his eyes grew to an endless, hopeless vista.

"Can't you put it together yet, Felix?"

"No sir."

He smiled and reached over to pat my forearm. There was something very calming about this gesture.

"To answer one of your questions," he said. "I once saved the life of the daughter of a man who is very influential at the St. Botolph Hospital."

"So?"

"Botolph funds Oberman's Sanitarium. I called this man and asked him to intervene. A price was set and there you are."

"I thought all you wanted me to do was take notes," I said, exhausted by the stretch of Lawless's reach.

"Tonight we'll go to a place I know across the river and tomorrow we'll come back to clear it all up." He reached in his pocket and came out with two dollar bills. "Oh. I seem to be a little short. Do you have any cash, son?"

"What about that big fat wallet you paid the nurse from?"

"I only had what I needed for the bribe. Don't you have some money left from that IOU you left me?"

I paid the bill and we left.

There was a motorboat waiting for us off a dilapidated pier across the West Side Highway. Because there were no stairs we had to jump down onto the launch, which then took us up river and deposited us at strange river inn on the Jersey side of the Hudson.

The inn had its own small dock. The boat captain, who was dark-skinned and utterly silent, let us off there. The key to the door was in a coffee can nailed to a wall. Lawless brought us in an area that was at least partially submerged in the River.

There was no one else in residence, at least no one there that I could see. The door Lawless opened led to a circular room that had four closed doors and led to an open hallway.

"Room two is yours," the anarchist told me. "Breakfast will be at the end of the hall when you wake up."

The bed was bunklike but very comfortable. Maybe the drug I'd been given before was still in effect but whatever the circumstance I was asleep as soon as I lay down.

19

The sunrise over Manhattan was magnificent. It sparkled on the water and shone brightly in my little cockleshell room. For almost the first full minute of consciousness I forgot my problems.

The respite was soon over, however. By the time I sat up anxiety was already clouding my mind. I dressed quickly. The hall outside my door led to a wide room under a low roof that was dominated by an irregularly shaped table—set for two.

"Good morning, Felix."

Archibald Lawless was eating scrambled eggs. A small Asian woman sat on a small stool against the wall. When I entered the room she stood up and pulled out the seat next to the anarchist. She nodded for me to sit and when I did so she scuttled out of the room.

"Mr. Lawless."

"Don't look so sad, son. Today all of our problems will be solved."

"Where are we?" I asked.

"Oh," he said, half smiling, looking like the main deity of some lost Buddhist tribe that found itself marooned in Africa an eon ago. "This is a halfway house. One of many such places where certain unpopular foreign dignitaries and agents come when they have to do business in America."

"Like who?" I asked.

"Militants, dethroned dictators, communist sympathizers, even anarchists have stayed here. Presidents and kings unpopular with current American regimes have slept in the same bed that you have, waiting to meet with clandestine mediators or diplomats from the UN."

"But there's no security."

"None that you've seen," Lawless said, bearing that saintly mien. "But there's enough protection close at hand to fend off an NYPD swat team."

"You're joking," I said.

"All right," he replied. "Have it your way."

The small woman returned with a plate of eggs and herring, a small bowl of rice and a mug full of smoky flavored tea. After serving me she returned to her perch against the wall.

I ate for a while. Lawless looked out of the window at Manhattan.

"So at the office you look at New Jersey and here you look at New York."

He cackled and then laughed. He grabbed my neck with his powerful hand and said, "I like you, boy. You know how to make me laugh."

"Who do you plan to kill today?"

He laughed again.

"I talked to your girlfriend last night," he said.

"Who?" I wondered if he had somehow gotten in touch with Sharee.

"Lana," he said articulating her name as an opera singer might in preparation for singing it later on. "She and Mr. Lamarr practised being engaged before she seduced Strangman."

"Okay."

"He told her things."

"What things?"

"People he trusted . . . places where certain transactions were to transpire."

"And where might that be?" I asked, sucked into the rhythm of his improvisational operetta.

"Today we go to Peninsula Hotel," he said. "There all of our problems will come to an end."

We exited the Refugee Inn (Lawless's term for it) by climbing a steep trail which led to a dirt path that became a paved lane after a quarter mile or so. There Derek was waiting for us. He drove off without asking for a destination.

On the way Lawless talked to me about my duties as his scribe. I was tired of arguing with him, and just a little frightened after seeing how easily he killed the assassin Wayne Sacorliss, and so I let him go on without contradiction.

A block away from the hotel I began to get nervous.

"What are we going to do here?" I asked.

"Have breakfast."

"We just had breakfast."

"The sacrifices we must make for the movement," he said. "Sometimes you have to wallow with the fat cats and follow their lead. Here, put these on."

He handed me a pair of glasses that had thick black rims and a blond wig.

"What are these for?"

"You're going to be incognito."

I donned the glasses and wig because I had already learned that there was logic to every move that my would-be employer made. I also half believed that the outlandish getup would get us thrown out of the hotel.

We entered the restaurant at about ten-thirty. No one gave me a second look.

When Lawless introduced himself the maître d' guided us to a table in an isolated corner of the main dining room. Lawless put himself in a seat with his back to rest of the room. I was seated in an alcove, hidden from view by the bauguette.

He ordered salmon hash with shirred eggs and I had the Marscapone pancakes with a side of apple smoked bacon.

After the breakfast was served I said, "I'm not going to work for you, you know."

"I know that you don't expect to take the job but the day is young."

"No. I'm not working for you under any condition. I don't even know what we're doing now. How can I take a job where I don't even know where I'll wake up in the morning?"

"You'd rather have a job where you'll know where you'll be every day for the rest of your life?" he asked.

"No. Of course not, but, I mean I don't want to be involved with criminals and dirty politics."

"You're the one who said that he always pays his taxes, Felix," he said. "That makes you a part of an elite criminal and political class. If you buy gasoline or knitted sweaters or even bananas then you belong to the greatest crime family on Earth."

I don't know why I argued with him. I had been around people like him ever since college. *Politico dingbats* is what my father calls them. People who see conspiracies in our economic system, people who believe America is actually set against the notion of liberty.

I talked about the Constitution. He talked about the millions dead in Africa, Cambodia, Vietnam, and Nagasaki. I talked about the freedom of speech. He came back with the millions of dark-skinned men and women who spend most of their lives in prison. I talked about international terrorism. He brushed that off and concentrated on the embargos imposed on Iraq, Iran, Cuba, and North Korea.

I was about to bring out the big guns: the American peoples and the part they played in World War Two. But just then a familiar man came up and sat down at our table.

"Right on time, Ray," Archibald Lawless said.

Our guest was dressed in a dark blue suit with a white shirt held together at the cuffs by sapphire studs. *Raymond*, I supposed his first name was. The only title I knew him by was Captain Delgado.

"Archie," he said. "Felix. What's up?"

The way he said my name was respectful, as if I deserved a place at the table. As much as I wanted to deny it, I liked that feeling.

"Two tables over to your right," Lawless told the police captain. "A man and a woman talking over caviar and scrambled eggs."

I leaned over and slanted my eyes to see them. Through the clear glass frames of my disguise I recognized Valerie Lox, the Madison Avenue real estate agent. The whole time we had been talking she was there meeting with a man who was unknown to me.

She was wearing a red Chanel suit and an orange scarf. I'd never seen the man she was with. He was porcine and yet handsome. His movements were self-assured to the degree where he almost seemed careless.

"You were recently made aware of a diamond theft, were you not, Captain Delgado?" Lawless asked.

"Are you telling me or digging?" the cop asked back.

"Red diamonds," Lawless replied. "Millions of dollars' worth. A syndicate represented by Lionel Strangman reported it to their insurance company."

"You have my attention."

"Is Felix still being sought in connection with the murder of Henry Lansman?"

"Until we find another candidate."

"Wait," I said. "Why would you even think of me?"

Delgado shrugged but said nothing.

"The boy has a right to know why he's being sought," Archibald said.

"The gems," the police captain said as if it were patently obvious. "A special unit started investigating Lamarr as soon as the theft was reported. They had Lansman, Brexel, Cornell, and Ms. Lox over there under surveillance. There was a tap on her phone. When she called Cornell we picked up your name. Then when you were photographed at the scene of Lansman's murder you became a suspect."

"Why not Sacorliss?" I asked.

"He's out of bounds," Delgado said. Works as an informant for the FBI."

"Regardless," Lawless said. "Sacorliss is your killer."

"Who does he work for?" Delgado asked.

"As you indicated," Lawless said with a sense of the dramatic in his tone, "the same people that you work for. He also killed Benny Lamarr and Kenneth Cornell. If you look into the records of those deaths you will find that they have disappeared. Gone to Arizona, I hear."

"Fuckin' meatheads," Delgado muttered.

"I agree," Lawless said. "You have another problem however."

"What's that?"

"The man sitting with Ms. Lox is Rudolph Bickell, one of the richest men in Canada. She is passing the diamonds to him. She may have already done so."

"You want me to arrest the richest man in Canada on your say-so?"

"It's a toss-up, my friend. Take the plunge and maybe you'll lose everything. Don't take it and pass up the chance of a lifetime."

Lawless gestured for the bill and then said to Delgado, "You can pay for our meal, officer. Because even just the arrest of Wayne Sacorliss will keep you in good standing with your superiors.

"Come on, Felix," he said then.

And he left without paying another bill.

20

Even the *Wall Street Journal* covered the arrest of the billionaire Rudolph Bickell. They also asked how the mysterious entrepreneur was able to make bail and flee the country within three hours of his arrest at the posh Peninsula Hotel in New York City. Bickell's spokesperson in Toronto told reporters that the industrialist had no knowledge that the diamonds he was purchasing were stolen; that there was no law against acquiring the gemstones from the legal representative of a diamond dealer. Valerie Lox, who *was* in jail, was working for a man named Benny Lamarr who had died in an unrelated auto accident.

The *Journal* didn't cover the murder of optical materials dealer Wayne Sacorliss. I had to read about that in the Metro Section of *The New York Times*. The police had no motive for the crime but they had not ruled out theft. It seemed that Sacorliss was known to carry large sums of cash.

No one connected Sacorliss with Lamarr.

There were no policemen waiting at my door either.

The next morning at five-fifty I was at the front desk of the Tessla building marveling bleary eyed at the saintliness of Joan of Arc.

"Mr. Orlean," a young red-headed guard said.

"How do you know my name?"

"Mr. Lawless gave us a picture of you so that we'd know to let you in even if you came in after five fifty-five."

He answered the door before I knocked. That morning he wore white overalls and a bloodred shirt. At his gesture I went into his office and sat on the tree trunk I'd used a few days before.

"What was it all about?" I asked him.

"That why you're here, Felix?"

"Yes sir."

"You want to know why," he said with a smile. "It bothers you to sit alone in your room thinking that the papers might have gotten it wrong, that the police might be covering up a crime. It's troubling that you can be exonerated from suspicion in a murder case with a few words over an expensive breakfast in midtown Manhattan. That's not the world you thought you were living in."

If I were superstitious I might have believed that he was a mind reader. As it was, I thought that he had incredible logical and intuitive faculties.

"Yes," I said, "but there's something else."

"First," he said, "let me tell you what I know."

He sat back in his chair and brought his hands together in front of his face as if in Christian prayer.

"There was, in the works of Agineau Armaments, a shipment being readied for delivery in Ecuador at the end of next month. The company slated to receive the shipment is a dummy corporation owned by a conservative plantation owner in Venezuela. It's not hard to see where the shipment is bound for and who will use the guns."

"So Bickell is funding conservative guerrillas in Venezuela?" I asked.

"Bickell wanted the diamonds. Sacorliss wanted to fund the revolution."

"Why?"

"That, my friend, is an argument that we will have over and over again. For my money Sacorliss is a well-trained operative of the United States government. His job was to plan a robbery set to fund our clandestine interests in South America. You probably believe that it isn't such a far-reaching conspiratorial act. Only time, and blood, will tell."

"What about Valerie Lox and Lana Drexel?"

"Lox was released from jail. She claimed that she knew nothing about stolen gems, that Lamarr had always been a reputable dealer. The prosecutors decided to believe her which makes me believe that she is also a government operative. I sent Drexel her money. She's moving to Hollywood. I've been trying to decipher the code of Sacorliss's computer. One day I'll succeed and prove to you that I'm right. All we have to discuss now are the final terms of your employment."

"What do you mean?" I asked. "You don't expect that I'm going to come work for you after what I've been through."

"Sure I do."

"Why?"

"Because of your aunt, of course. You'll agree to work for me for a specified amount of time and I will agree to do what your father refused to do, free your aunt from jail."

The hairs on the back of my neck rose up then. I hadn't even considered this option until the middle of the night before. My face must have exposed my surprise.

"I need you, Felix," Lawless said. "You complete a faulty circuit in my head. You give me the three years that your aunt has left on her sentence and I will make sure that she's out of the joint by Sunday next."

"I still won't be involved in any crimes," I said.

"Agreed. I won't knowingly put you in the position of breaking the law. You will write down everything of import that I say, regardless of your own opinions. I in turn will open your eyes to a whole new world. As a journalist you will learn more from me than from a thousand seminars."

There was no reason for me to argue.

"Okay," I said. "But I have two needs and one question."

"And what might those be?"

"First is salary."

"Forty-two thousand dollars a year payable from a fund set up by Auchschlous, Anterbe, and Grenell, the world's largest insurers of rare gems. They prepared the account at my behest."

"Two," I said, "is that you agree not to lie to me. If I ask you a question you answer to the best of your ability."

"Agreed," Lawless replied, "depending upon circumstances. It might be that the truth would be giving away someone else's secret and that I have no right to do."

"Okay. Fine. Then I agree. Three years terminable if you decide I can't do the job or if you break your word to me. All of course contingent upon the release of my aunt Alberta."

"You had a question," Lawless reminded me.

"Oh. Yeah. It didn't have to do with our contract."

"Ask anyway."

"Who was the woman who came to your apartment door, the one in Harlem? I think she said her name was Maddie."

"Oh. No one. She had nothing to do with our business."

"But who was she?" I asked.

"My fiancée," he said. "She's been looking for me for a couple of years now."

———

I'm still in school, still out of contact with my parents. My aunt Alberta was freed from jail on a technicality that a colleague of my father turned up. She's coming to live in New York.

I work for the anarchist at least four days a week. We argue almost every day I'm there. I still think he's crazy but I've learned that doesn't always mean he's wrong.

LAWRENCE BLOCK

There are two kinds of stylists: the show-off who wants to be congratulated every time he turns a nice phrase and the kind who quietly turns a nice phrase but just gets on with the story. **Lawrence Block** is one of the latter. Even at the outset of his career, when he was turning out books at a furious pace, he managed to bring elegance and taste to even minor assignments, particularly with a knowing, wry take on the relationships and interactions between his characters: men with women, men with men, fathers and sons, husbands and wives. His hard work paid off. Not only is he one of the premier crime novelists of our time—with two bestselling series: the Matt Scudder novels (dark), including *Eight Million Ways to Die*, *The Devil Knows You're Dead*, and the Edgar-winning *A Dance at the Slaughterhouse*; and the Bernie Rhodenbarr mysteries (humorous), including *The Burglar Who Thought He Was Bogart* and *The Burglar Who Traded Ted Williams*—he is also one of our most accomplished short story writers. No wonder the Mystery Writers of America hailed him as one of the Grand Masters. Recently he turned to editing books, with seven stellar anthologies published: *Master's Choice, Vol. 1 and 2*, *Opening Shots, Vol. 1 and 2*, *Speaking of Lust* and *Speaking of Greed*, and the MWA anthology *Blood on Their Hands*. His latest novels are *All the Flowers Are Dying*, a Matthew Scudder novel, and another Bernie Rhodenbarr mystery, *The Burglar on the Prowl*.

KELLER'S ADJUSTMENT

Lawrence Block

Keller, waiting for the traffic light to turn from red to green, wondered what had happened to the world. The traffic light wasn't the problem. There'd been traffic lights for longer than he could remember, longer than he'd been alive. For almost as long as there had been automobiles, he supposed, although the automobile had clearly come first, and would in fact have necessitated the traffic light. At first they'd have made do without them, he supposed, and then, when there were enough cars around for them to start slamming into one another, someone would have figured out that some form of control was necessary, some device to stop east-west traffic while allowing north-south traffic to proceed, and then switching.

He could imagine an early motorist fulminating against the new regimen. *Whole world's going to hell. They're taking our rights away one after another. Light turns red because some damn timer tells it to turn red, a man's supposed to stop what he's doing and hit the brakes. Don't matter if there ain't another car around for fifty miles, he's gotta stop and stand there like a goddam fool until the light turns green and tells him he can go again. Who wants to live in a country like that? Who wants to bring children into a world where that kind of crap goes on?*

A horn sounded, jarring Keller abruptly from the early days of the twentieth century to the early days of the twenty-first. The light, he noted, had turned from red to green, and the fellow in the SUV just behind him felt a need to bring this fact to Keller's attention. Keller, without feeling much in the way of actual irritation or anger, allowed himself a moment of imagination in which he shifted into park, engaged the emergency brake, got out of the car and walked back to the SUV, whose driver would already have begun to regret leaning on the horn. Even as the man (pig-faced and jowly in Keller's fantasy) was reaching for the button to lock the door, Keller was opening the door, taking hold of the man (sweating now, stammering, making simultaneous threats and excuses) by the shirtfront, yanking him out of the car, sending him sprawling on the pavement. Then, while the man's child (no, make it his wife, a fat shrew with dyed hair and rheumy eyes) watched in horror, Keller bent from the waist and dispatched the man with a movement learned from the Burmese master U Minh U, one in which the adept's hands barely appeared to touch the subject, but death, while indescribably painful, was virtually instantaneous.

Keller, satisfied by the fantasy, drove on. Behind him, the driver of the SUV—an unaccompanied young woman, Keller now noted, her hair secured by a bandana, and a sack of groceries on the seat beside her—followed along for half a block, then turned off to the right, seemingly unaware of her close brush with death.

How you do go on, he thought.

It was all the damned driving. Before everything went to hell, he wouldn't have had to drive clear across the country. He'd have taken a cab to JFK and caught a flight to Phoenix, where he'd have rented a car, driven it around for the day or two it would take to do the job, then turned it in and flown back to New York. In and out, case closed, and he could get on with his life.

And leave no traces behind, either. They made you show ID to get on the plane, they'd been doing that for a few years now, but it didn't have to be terribly good ID. Now they all but fingerprinted you before they let you board, and they went through your checked baggage and gave your carry-on luggage a lethal dose of radiation. God help you if you had a nail clipper on your key ring.

He hadn't flown at all since the new security procedures had gone into effect, and he didn't know that he'd ever get on a plane again. Business travel was greatly reduced, he'd read, and he could understand why. A business traveler would rather hop in his car and drive five hundred miles than get to the airport two hours early and go through all the hassles the new system imposed. It was bad enough if your business consisted of meeting with groups of salesmen and giving them pep talks. If you were in Keller's line of work, well, it was out of the question.

Keller rarely traveled other than for business, but sometimes he'd go somewhere for a stamp auction, or because it was the middle of a New York winter and he felt the urge to lie in the sun somewhere. He supposed he could still fly on such occasions, showing valid ID and clipping his nails before departure, but would he want to? Would it still be pleasure travel if you had to go through all that in order to get there?

He felt like that imagined motorist, griping about red lights. *Hell, if that's what they're gonna make me do, I'll just walk. Or I'll stay home. That'll show them!*

It all changed, of course, on a September morning, when a pair of airliners flew into the twin towers of the World Trade Center. Keller, who lived on First Avenue not far from the UN building, had not been home at the time. He was in Miami, where he had already spent a week, getting ready to kill a man named Rubén Olivares. Olivares was a Cuban, and an important figure in one of the Cuban exile groups, but Keller wasn't sure that was why someone had been willing to spend a substantial amount of money to have him killed. It was possible, certainly, that he was a thorn in the side of the Castro government, and that someone had decided it would be safer and more cost-effective to hire the work done than to send a team of agents from Havana. It was also possible that Olivares had turned out to be a spy for Havana, and it was his fellow exiles who had it in for him.

Then too, he might be sleeping with the wrong person's wife, or muscling in on the wrong person's drug trade. With a little investigative work, Keller might have managed to find out who wanted Olivares dead, and why, but he'd long since determined that such considerations were none of his business. What difference did it make? He had a job to do, and all he had to do was do it.

Monday night, he'd followed Olivares around, watched him eat dinner at a steakhouse in Coral Gables, then tagged along when Olivares and two of his dinner companions hit a couple of titty bars in Miami Beach. Olivares left with one of the dancers, and Keller tailed him to the woman's apartment and waited for him to come out. After an hour and a half, Keller decided the man was spending the night. Keller, who'd watched lights go on and off in the apartment house, was reasonably certain he knew which apartment the couple was occupying, and didn't think it would prove difficult to get into the building. He thought about going in and getting it over with. It was too late to catch a flight to New York, it was the middle of the night, but he could get the work done and stop at his motel to shower and collect his luggage, then go straight to the airport and catch an early morning flight to New York.

Or he could sleep late and fly home sometime in the early afternoon. Several airlines flew from New York to Florida, and there were flights all day long. Miami International was not his favorite airport—it was not anybody's favorite airport—but he could skip it if he wanted, turning in his rental car at Fort Lauderdale or West Palm Beach and flying home from there.

No end of options, once the work was done.

But he'd have to kill the woman, the topless dancer.

He'd do that if he had to, but he didn't like the idea of killing people just because they were in the way. A higher body count drew more police and media attention, but that wasn't it, nor was the notion of slaughtering the innocent. How did he know the woman was innocent? For that matter, who was to say Olivares was guilty of anything?

Later, when he thought about it, it seemed to him that the deciding factor was purely physical. He'd slept poorly the night before, rising early and spending the whole day driving around unfamiliar streets. He was tired, and he didn't much feel like forcing a door and climbing a flight of stairs and killing one person, let alone two. And suppose she had a roommate, and suppose the roommate had a boyfriend, and—

He went back to his motel, took a long hot shower, and went to bed.

When he woke up he didn't turn on the TV, but went across the street to the place where he'd been having his breakfast every morning. He walked in the door and saw that something was different. They had a television set on the back counter, and everybody was staring at it. He watched for a few minutes, then picked up a container of coffee and took it back to his room. He sat in front of his own TV and watched the same scenes, over and over and over.

If he'd done his work the night before, he realized, he might have been in the air when it happened. Or maybe not, because he'd probably have decided to get some sleep instead, so he'd be right where he was, in his motel room, watching the plane fly into the building. The only certain difference was that Rubén Olivares, who as things stood was probably watching the same footage everybody else in America was watching (except that he might well be watching it on a Spanish-language station)—well, Olivares wouldn't be watching TV. Nor would he be on it. A garden-variety Miami homicide wasn't worth airtime on a day like this, not even if the deceased was of some importance in the Cuban exile community, not even if he'd been murdered in the apartment of a topless dancer, with her own death a part of the package. A newsworthy item any other day, but not on this day. There was only one sort of news today, one topic with endless permutations, and Keller watched it all day long.

It was Wednesday before it even occurred to him to call Dot, and late Thursday before he finally got a call through to her in White Plains. "I've been wondering about you, Keller," she said. "There are all these planes on the ground in Newfoundland, they were in the air when it happened and got rerouted there, and God knows when they're gonna let them come home. I had the feeling you might be there."

"In Newfoundland?"

"The local people are taking the stranded passengers into their homes," she said. "Making them welcome, giving them cups of beef bouillon and ostrich sandwiches, and—"

"Ostrich sandwiches?"

"Whatever. I just pictured you there, Keller, making the best of a bad situation, which I guess is what you're doing in Miami. God knows when they're going to let you fly home. Have you got a car?"

"A rental."

"Well, hang on to it," she said. "Don't give it back, because the car rental agencies are emptied out, with so many people stranded and trying to drive home. Maybe that's what you ought to do."

"I was thinking about it," he said. "But I was also thinking about, you know. The guy."

"Oh, him."

"I don't want to say his name, but—"

"No, don't."

"The thing is, he's still, uh . . ."

"Doing what he always did."

"Right."

"Instead of doing like John Brown."

"Huh?"

"Or John Brown's body," Dot said. "Moldering in the grave, as I recall."

"Whatever *moldering* means."

"We can probably guess, Keller, if we put our minds to it. You're wondering is it still on, right?"

"It seems ridiculous even thinking about it," he said. "But on the other hand—"

"On the other hand," she said, "they sent half the money. I'd just as soon not have to give it back."

"No."

"In fact," she said, "I'd just as soon have them send the other half. If they're the ones to call it off, we keep what they sent. And if they say it's still on, well, you're already in Miami, aren't you? Sit tight, Keller, while I make a phone call."

Whoever had wanted Olivares dead had not changed his mind as a result of several thousand deaths fifteen hundred miles away. Keller, thinking about it, couldn't see why he should be any less sanguine about the prospect of killing Olivares than he had been Monday night. On the television news, there was a certain amount of talk about the possible positive effects of the tragedy. New Yorkers, someone suggested, would be brought closer together, aware as never before of the bonds created by their common humanity.

Did Keller feel a bond with Rubén Olivares of which he'd been previously unaware? He thought about it and decided he did not. If anything, he was faintly aware of a grudging resentment against the man. If Olivares had spent less time over dinner and hurried through the foreplay of the titty bar, if he'd gone directly to the topless dancer's apartment and left the premises in the throes of post-coital bliss, Keller could have taken him out in time to catch the last flight back to the city. He might have been in his own apartment when the attack came.

And what earthly difference would that have made? None, he

had to concede. He'd have watched the hideous drama unfold on his own television set, just as he'd watched on the motel's unit, and he'd have been no more capable of influencing events whatever set he watched.

Olivares, with his steak dinners and topless dancers, made a poor surrogate for the heroic cops and firemen, the doomed office workers. He was, Keller conceded, a fellow member of the human race. If all men were brothers, a possibility Keller, an only child, was willing to entertain, well, brothers had been killing one another for a good deal longer than Keller had been on the job. If Olivares was Abel, Keller was willing to be Cain.

If nothing else, he was grateful for something to do.

And Olivares made it easy. All over America, people were writing checks and inundating blood banks, trying to do something for the victims in New York. Cops and firemen and ordinary citizens were piling into cars and heading north and east, eager to join in the rescue efforts. Olivares, on the other hand, went on leading his life of self-indulgence, going to an office in the morning, making a circuit of bars and restaurants in the afternoon and early evening, and finishing up with rum drinks in a room full of bare breasts.

Keller tagged him for three days and three nights, and by the third night he'd decided not to be squeamish about the topless dancer. He waited outside the titty bar, until a call of nature led him into the bar, past Olivares's table (where the man was chatting up three silicone-enhanced young ladies) and on to the men's room. Standing at the urinal, Keller wondered what he'd do if the Cuban took all three of them home.

He washed his hands, left the restroom, and saw Olivares counting out bills to settle his tab. All three women were still at the table, and playing up to him, one clutching his arm and leaning her breasts against it, the others just as coquettish. Keller, who'd been ready to sacrifice one bystander, found himself drawing the line at three.

But wait—Olivares was on his feet, his body language suggesting he was excusing himself for a moment. And yes, he was on his way to the men's room, clearly aware of the disadvantage of attempting a night of love on a full bladder.

Keller slipped into the room ahead of him, ducked into an empty stall. There was an elderly gentleman at the urinal, talking soothingly in Spanish to himself, or perhaps to his prostate. Olivares entered the room, stood at the adjoining urinal, and began chattering in Spanish to the older man, who spoke slow sad sentences in response.

Shortly after arriving in Miami, Keller had gotten hold of a gun, a .22-caliber revolver. It was a small gun with a short barrel, and fit easily in his pocket. He took it out now, wondering if the noise would carry.

If the older gentleman left first, Keller might not need the gun. But if Olivares finished first, Keller couldn't let him leave, and would have to do them both, and that would mean using the gun, and a minimum of two shots. He watched them over the top of the stall, wishing that something would happen before some other drunken voyeur felt a need to pee. Then the older man finished up, tucked himself in, and headed for the door.

And paused at the threshold, returning to wash his hands, and saying something to Olivares, who laughed heartily at it, whatever it was. Keller, who'd returned the gun to his pocket, took it out again, and replaced it a moment later when the older gentleman left. Olivares waited until the door closed after him, then produced a little blue glass bottle and a tiny spoon. He treated each of his cavernous nostrils to two quick hits of what Keller could only presume to be cocaine, then returned the bottle and spoon to his pocket and turned to face the sink.

Keller burst out of the stall. Olivares, washing his hands, evidently couldn't hear him with the water running; in any event he didn't react before Keller reached him, one hand cupping his jowly chin, the other taking hold of his greasy mop of hair. Keller had never studied the martial arts, not even from a Burmese with an improbable name, but he'd been doing this sort of thing long enough to have learned a trick or two. He broke Olivares's neck and was dragging him across the floor to the stall he'd just vacated when, damn it to hell, the door burst open and a little man in shirtsleeves got halfway to the urinal before he suddenly realized what he'd just seen. His eyes widened, his jaw dropped, and Keller got him before he could make a sound.

The little man's bladder, unable to relieve itself in life, could not be denied in death. Olivares, having emptied his bladder in his last moments of life, voided his bowels. The men's room, no garden spot to begin with, stank to the heavens. Keller stuffed both bodies into one stall and got out of there in a hurry, before some other son of a bitch could rush in and join the party.

Half an hour later he was heading north on I-95. Somewhere north of Stuart he stopped for gas, and in the men's room—empty, spotless, smelling of nothing but pine-scented disinfectant—he put his hands against the smooth white tiles and vomited. Hours later, at a rest area just across the Georgia line, he did so again.

He couldn't blame it on the killing. It had been a bad idea, lurking in the men's room. The traffic was too heavy, with all those drinkers and cocaine-sniffers. The stench of the corpses he'd left there, on top of the reek that had permeated the room to start with, could well have turned his stomach, but it would have done so then, not a hundred miles away when it no longer existed outside of his memory.

Some members of his profession, he knew, typically threw up after a piece of work, just as some veteran actors never failed to vomit before a performance. Keller had known a man once, a cheerfully cold-blooded little murderer with dainty little-girl wrists and a way of holding a cigarette between his thumb and forefinger. The man would chatter about his work, excuse himself, throw up discreetly into a basin, and resume his conversation in midsentence.

A shrink would probably argue that the body was expressing a revulsion which the mind was unwilling to acknowledge, and that sounded about right to Keller. But it didn't apply to him, because he'd never been one for puking. Even early on, when he was new to the game and hadn't found ways to deal with it, his stomach had remained serene.

This particular incident had been unpleasant, even chaotic, but he could if pressed recall others that had been worse.

But there was a more conclusive argument, it seemed to him. Yes, he'd thrown up outside of Stuart, and again in Georgia, and he'd very likely do so a few more times before he reached New York. But it hadn't begun with the killings.

He'd thrown up every couple of hours ever since he sat in front of his television set and watched the towers fall.

A week or so after he got back, there was a message on his answering machine. Dot, wanting him to call. He checked his watch, decided it was too early. He made himself a cup of coffee, and when he'd finished it he dialed the number in White Plains.

"Keller," she said. "When you didn't call back, I figured you were out late. And now you're up early."

"Well," he said.

"Why don't you get on a train, Keller? My eyes are sore, and I figure you're a sight for them."

"What's the matter with your eyes?"

"Nothing," she said. "I was trying to express myself in an original fashion, and it's a mistake I won't make again in a hurry. Come see me, why don't you?"

"Now?"

"Why not?"

"I'm beat," he said. "I was up all night, I need to get to sleep."

"What were you . . . never mind, I don't need to know. All right, I'll tell you what. Sleep all you want and come out for dinner. I'll order something from the Chinese. Keller? You're not answering me."

"I'll come out sometime this afternoon," he said.

He went to bed, and early that afternoon he caught a train to White Plains and a cab from the station. She was on the porch of the big old Victorian on Taunton Place, with a pitcher of iced tea and two glasses on the tin-topped table. "Look," she said, pointing to the lawn. "I swear the trees are dropping their leaves earlier than usual this year. What's it like in New York?"

"I haven't really been paying attention."

"There was a kid who used to come around to rake them, but I guess he must have gone to college or something. What happens if you don't rake the leaves, Keller? You happen to know?"

He didn't.

"And you're not hugely interested, I can see that. There's something different about you, Keller, and I've got a horrible feeling I know what it is. You're not in love, are you?"

"In love?"

"Well, are you? Out all night, and then when you get home all you can do is sleep. Who's the lucky girl, Keller?"

He shook his head. "No girl," he said. "I've been working nights."

"Working? What the hell do you mean, working?"

He let her drag it out of him. A day or two after he got back to the city and turned in his rental car, he'd heard something on the news and went to one of the Hudson River piers, where they were enlisting volunteers to serve food for the rescue workers at Ground Zero. Around ten every evening they'd all get together at the pier, then sail down the river and board another ship anchored near the site. Top chefs supplied the food, and Keller and his fellows dished it out to men who'd worked up prodigious appetites laboring at the smoldering wreckage.

"My God," Dot said. "Keller, I'm trying to picture this. You stand there with a big spoon and fill their plates for them? Do you wear an apron?"

"Everybody wears an apron."

"I bet you look cute in yours. I don't mean to make fun, Keller. What you're doing's a good thing, and of course you'd wear an apron. You wouldn't want to get marinara sauce all over your shirt. But it seems strange to me, that's all."

"It's something to do," he said.

"It's heroic."

He shook his head. "There's nothing heroic about it. It's like working in a diner, dishing out food. The men we feed, they work long shifts doing hard physical work and breathing in all that smoke. That's heroic, if anything is. Though I'm not sure there's any point to it."

"What do you mean?"

"Well, they call them rescue workers," he said, "but they're not rescuing anybody, because there's nobody to rescue. Everybody's dead."

She said something in response but he didn't hear it. "It's the same as with the blood," he said. "The first day, everybody mobbed the hospitals, donating blood for the wounded. But it turned out there weren't any wounded. People either got out of the buildings or they didn't. If they got out, they were okay. If they didn't, they're dead. All that blood people donated? They've been throwing it out."

"It seems like a waste."

"It's all a waste," he said, and frowned. "Anyway, that's what I do every night. I dish out food, and they try to rescue dead people. That way we all keep busy."

"The longer I know you," Dot said, "the more I realize I don't."

"Don't what?"

"Know you, Keller. You never cease to amaze me. Somehow I never pictured you as Florence Nightingale."

"I'm not nursing anybody. All I do is feed them."

"Betty Crocker, then. Either way, it seems like a strange role for a sociopath."

"You think I'm a sociopath?"

"Well, isn't that part of the job description, Keller? You're a hit man, a contract killer. You leave town and kill strangers and get paid for it. How can you do that without being a sociopath?"

He thought about it.

"Look," she said, "I didn't mean to bring it up. It's just a word, and who even knows what it means? Let's talk about something else, like why I called you and got you to come out here."

"Okay."

"Actually," she said, "there's two reasons. First of all, you've got money coming. Miami, remember?"

"Oh, right."

She handed him an envelope. "I thought you'd want this," she said, "although it couldn't have been weighing on your mind, because you never asked about it."

"I hardly thought about it."

"Well, why would you want to think about blood money while you were busy doing good works? But you can probably find a use for it."

"No question."

"You can always buy stamps with it. For your collection."

"Sure."

"It must be quite a collection by now."

"It's coming along."

"I'll bet it is. The other reason I called, Keller, is somebody called me."

"Oh?"

She poured herself some more iced tea, took a sip. "There's work," she said. "If you want it. In Portland, something to do with labor unions."

"Which Portland?"

"You know," she said, "I keep forgetting there's one in Maine, but there is, and I suppose they've got their share of labor problems there, too. But this is Portland, Oregon. As a matter of fact, it's Beaverton, but I think it's a suburb. The area code's the same as Portland."

"Clear across the country," he said.

"Just a few hours in a plane."

They looked at each other. "I can remember," he said, "when all you did was step up to the counter and tell them where you wanted to go. You counted out bills, and they were perfectly happy to be paid in cash. You had to give them a name, but you could make it up on the spot, and the only way they asked for identification was if you tried to pay them by check."

"The world's a different place now, Keller."

"They didn't even have metal detectors," he remembered, "or scanners. Then they brought in metal detectors, but the early ones didn't work all the way down to the ground. I knew a man who used to stick a gun into his sock and walk right onto the plane with it. If they ever caught him at it, I never heard about it."

"I suppose you could take a train."

"Or a clipper ship," he said. "Around the Horn."

"What's the matter with the Panama Canal? Metal detectors?" She finished the tea in her glass, heaved a sigh. "I think you answered my question. I'll tell Portland we have to pass."

After dinner she gave him a lift to the station and joined him on the platform to wait for his train. He broke the silence to ask her if she really thought he was a sociopath.

"Keller," she said, "it was just an idle remark, and I didn't mean anything by it. Anyway, I'm no psychologist. I'm not even sure what the word means."

"Someone who lacks a sense of right and wrong," he said. "He understands the difference but doesn't see how it applies to him personally. He lacks empathy, doesn't have any feeling for other people."

She considered the matter. "It doesn't sound like you," she said, "except when you're working. Is it possible to be a part-time sociopath?"

"I don't think so. I've done some reading on the subject. Case histories, that sort of thing. The sociopaths they write about, almost all of them have the same three things in their childhood background. Setting fires, torturing animals, and wetting the bed."

"You know, I heard that somewhere. Some TV program about FBI profilers and serial killers. Do you remember your childhood, Keller?"

"Most of it," he said. "I knew a woman once who claimed she could remember being born. I don't go back that far, and some of it's spotty, but I remember it pretty well. And I didn't do any of those three things. Torture animals? God, I loved animals. I told you about the dog I had."

"Nelson. No, sorry, that was the one you had a couple of years ago. You told me the name of the other one, but I can't remember it."

"Soldier."

"Soldier, right."

"I loved that dog," he said. "And I had other pets from time to time, the ways kids do. Goldfish, baby turtles. They all died."

"They always do, don't they?"

"I suppose so. I used to cry."

"When they died."

"When I was little. When I got older I took it more in stride, but it still made me sad. But torture them?"

"How about fires?"

"You know," he said, "when you talked about the leaves, and what happens if you don't rake them, I remembered raking leaves when I was a kid. It was one of the things I did to make money."

"You want to make twenty bucks here and now, there's a rake in the garage."

"What we used to do," he remembered, "was rake them into a pile at the curb, and then burn them. It's illegal nowadays, because of fire laws and air pollution, but back then it's what you were supposed to do."

"It was nice, the smell of burning leaves on the autumn air."

"And it was satisfying," he said. "You raked them up and put a match to them and they were gone. Those were the only fires I remember setting."

"I'd say you're oh-for-two. How'd you do at wetting the bed?"

"I never did, as far as I can recall."

"Oh-for-three. Keller, you're about as much of a sociopath as Albert Schweitzer. But if that's the case, how come you do what you do? Never mind, here's your train. Have fun dishing out the lasagna tonight. And don't torture any animals, you hear?"

Two weeks later he picked up the phone on his own and told her not to turn down jobs automatically. "Now you tell me," she said. "You at home? Don't go anywhere, I'll make a call and get back to you."

He sat by the phone, and picked it up when it rang. "I was afraid they'd found somebody by now," she said, "but we're in luck, if you want to call it that. They're sending us something by Airborne Express, which always sounds to me like paratroopers ready for battle. They swear I'll have it by nine tomorrow morning, but you'll just be getting home around then, won't you? Do you figure you can make the 2:04 from Grand Central? I'll pick you up at the station."

"There's a 10:08," he said. "Gets to White Plains a few minutes before eleven. If you're not there I'll figure you had to wait for the paratroopers, and I'll get a cab."

It was a cold, dreary day, with enough rain so that she needed to use the windshield wipers but not enough to keep the blades from squeaking. She put him at the kitchen table, poured him a cup of coffee, and let him read the notes she'd made and study the Polaroids that had come in the Airborne Express envelope, along with the initial payment in cash. He held up one of the pictures, which showed a man in his seventies, with a round face and a small white mustache, holding up a golf club as if in the hope that someone would take it from him.

He said the fellow didn't look much like a labor leader, and Dot shook her head. "That was Portland," she said. "This is Phoenix. Well, Scottsdale, and I bet it's nicer there today than it is here. Nicer than Portland, too, because I understand it always rains there. In Portland, I mean. It never rains in Scottsdale. I don't know what's the matter with me, I'm starting to sound like the Weather Channel. You could fly, you know. Not all the way, but to Denver, say."

"Maybe."

She tapped the photo with her fingernail. "Now according to them," she said, "the man's not expecting anything, and not taking any security precautions. Other hand, his life is a security precaution. He lives in a gated community."

"Sundowner Estates, it says here."

"There's an eighteen-hole golf course, with individual homes ranged around it. And each of them has a state-of-the-art home security system, but the only thing that ever triggers an alarm is when some clown hooks his tee shot through your living room picture window, because the only way into the compound is past a guard. No metal detector, and they don't confiscate your nail clippers, but you have to belong there for him to let you in."

"Does Mr. Egmont ever leave the property?"

"He plays golf every day. Unless it rains, and we've already established that it never does. He generally eats lunch at the clubhouse, they've got their own restaurant. He has a housekeeper who comes in a couple of times a week—they know her at the guard shack, I guess. Aside from that, he's all alone in his house. He probably gets invited out to dinner a lot. He's unattached, and there's always six women for every man in those Geezer Leisure communities. You're staring at his picture, and I bet I know why. He looks familiar, doesn't he?"

"Yes, and I can't think why."

"You ever play Monopoly?"

"By God, that's it," he said. "He looks like the drawing of the banker in Monopoly."

"It's the mustache," she said, "and the round face. Don't forget to pass Go, Keller. And collect two hundred dollars."

She drove him back to the train station, and because of the rain they waited in her car instead of on the platform. He said he'd pretty much stopped working on the food ship. She said she hadn't figured it was something he'd be doing for the rest of his life.

"They changed it," he said. "The Red Cross took it over. They do this all the time, their specialty's disaster relief, and they're pros at it, but it transformed the whole thing from a spontaneous New York affair into something impersonal. I mean, when we started we had name chefs knocking themselves out to feed these guys something they'd enjoy eating, and then the Red Cross took over and we were filling their plates with macaroni and cheese and chipped beef on toast. Overnight we went from Bobby Flay to Chef Boy-Ar-Dee."

"Took the joy out of it, did it?"

"Well, would you like to spend ten hours shifting scrap metal and collecting body parts and then tuck into something you'd expect to find in an army chow line? I got so I couldn't look them in the eye when I ladled the slop onto their plates. I skipped a night and felt guilty about it, and I went in the next night and felt worse, and I haven't been back since."

"You were probably ready to give it up, Keller."

"I don't know. I still felt good doing it, until the Red Cross showed up."

"But that's why you were there," she said. "To feel good."

"To help out."

She shook her head. "You felt good because you were helping out," she said, "but you kept coming back and doing it because it made you feel good."

"Well, I suppose so."

"I'm not impugning your motive, Keller. You're still a hero, as far as I'm concerned. All I'm saying is that volunteerism only goes so far. When it stops feeling good, it tends to run out of steam. That's when you need the professionals. They do their job because it's their job, and it doesn't matter whether they feel good about it or not. They buckle down and get it done. It may be macaroni and cheese, and the cheese may be Velveeta, but nobody winds up holding an empty plate. You see what I mean?"

"I guess so," Keller said.

Back in the city, he called one of the airlines, thinking he'd take Dot's suggestion and fly to Denver. He worked his way through their automated answering system, pressing numbers when prompted, and wound up on hold, because all of their agents were busy serving other customers. The music they played to pass the time was bad enough all by itself, but they kept interrupting it every fifteen seconds to tell him how much better off he'd be using their Web site. After a few minutes of this he called Hertz, and the phone was answered right away by a human being.

He picked up a Ford Taurus first thing the next morning and beat the rush hour traffic through the tunnel and onto the New Jersey Turnpike. He'd rented the car under his own name, showing his own driver's license and using his own American Express card, but he had a cloned card in another name that Dot had provided, and he used it in the motels where he stopped along the way.

It took him four long days to drive to Tucson. He would drive until he was hungry, or the car needed gas, or he needed a restroom, then get behind the wheel again and drive some more. When he got tired he'd find a motel and register under the name on his fake credit

card, take a shower, watch a little TV, and go to bed. He'd sleep until he woke up, and then he'd take another shower and get dressed
and look for someplace to have breakfast. And so on.

While he drove he played the radio until he couldn't stand it, then
turned it off until he couldn't stand the silence. By the third day the
solitude was getting to him, and he couldn't figure out why. He was
used to being alone, he lived his whole life alone, and he certainly
never had or wanted company while he was working. He seemed to
want it now, though, and at one point turned the car's radio to a talk
show on a clear-channel station in Omaha. People called in and dis-
agreed with the host, or a previous caller, or some schoolteacher
who'd given them a hard time in the fifth grade. Gun control was the
announced topic for the day, but the real theme, as far as Keller could
tell, was resentment, and there was plenty of it to go around.

Keller listened, fascinated at first, and before very long he
reached the point where he couldn't stand another minute of it. If
he'd had a gun handy, he might have put a bullet in the radio, but all
he did was switch it off.

The last thing he wanted, it turned out, was someone talking to
him. He had the thought, and realized a moment later that he'd not
only thought it but had actually spoken the words aloud. He was
talking to himself, and wondered—wondered in silence, thank
God—if this was something new. It was like snoring, he thought. If
you slept alone, how would you know if you did it? You wouldn't, not
unless you snored so loudly that you woke yourself up.

He started to reach for the radio, stopped himself before he
could turn it on again. He checked the speedometer, saw that the
cruise control was keeping the car at three miles an hour over the
posted speed limit. Without cruise control you found yourself going
faster or slower than you wanted to, wasting time or risking a ticket.
With it, you didn't have to think about how fast you were going. The
car did the thinking for you.

The next step, he thought, would be steering control. You got in
the car, keyed the ignition, set the controls, and leaned back and
closed your eyes. The car followed the turns in the road, and a system of sensors worked the brake when another car loomed in front of
you, swung out to pass when such action was warranted, and knew to
take the next exit when the gas gauge dropped below a certain level.

It sounded like science fiction, but no less so in Keller's boyhood than cruise control, or auto-response telephone answering systems, or a good ninety-five percent of the things he nowadays took for granted. Keller didn't doubt for a minute that right this minute some bright young man in Detroit or Osaka or Bremen was working on steering control. There'd be some spectacular head-on collisions before they got the bugs out of the system, but before long every car would have it, and the accident rate would plummet and the state troopers wouldn't have anybody to give tickets to, and everybody would be crazy about technology's newest breakthrough, except for a handful of cranks in England who were convinced you had more control and got better mileage the old-fashioned way.

Meanwhile, Keller kept both hands on the steering wheel.

Sundowner Estates, home of William Wallis Egmont, was in Scottsdale, an upscale suburb of Phoenix. Tucson, a couple hundred miles to the east, was as close as Keller wanted to bring the Taurus. He followed the signs to the airport and left the car in long-term parking. Over the years he'd left other cars in long-term parking, but they'd been other men's cars, with their owners stuffed in the trunk, and Keller, having no need to find the cars again, had gotten rid of the claim checks at the first opportunity. This time was different, and he found a place in his wallet for the check the gate attendant had supplied, and noted the lot section and the number of the parking space.

He went into the terminal, found the car rental counters, and picked up a Toyota Camry from Avis, using his fake credit card and a matching Pennsylvania driver's license. It took him a few minutes to figure out the cruise control. That was the trouble with renting cars, you had to learn a new system with every car, from lights and windshield wipers to cruise control and seat adjustment. Maybe he should have gone to the Hertz counter and picked up another Taurus. Was there an advantage in driving the same model car throughout? Was there a disadvantage that offset it, and was some intuitive recognition of that disadvantage what had led him to the Avis counter?

"You're thinking too much," he said, and realized he'd spoken the words aloud. He shook his head, not so much annoyed as amused, and a few miles down the road realized that what he wanted, what he'd been wanting all along, was not someone to talk to him but someone to listen.

A little ways past an exit ramp, a kid with a duffel bag had his thumb out, trying to hitch a ride. For the first time that he could recall, Keller had the impulse to stop for him. It was just a passing thought; if he'd had his foot on the gas, he'd have barely begun to ease up on the gas pedal before he'd overruled the thought and sped onward. Since he was running on cruise control, his foot didn't even move, and the hitchhiker slipped out of sight in the rearview mirror, unaware what a narrow escape he'd just had.

Because the only reason to pick him up was for someone to talk to, and Keller would have told him everything. And, once he'd done that, what choice would he have?

Keller could picture the kid, listening wide-eyed to everything Keller had to tell him. He pictured himself, his soul unburdened, grateful to the youth for listening, but compelled by circumstance to cover his tracks. He imagined the car gliding to a stop, imagined the brief struggle, imagined the body left in a roadside ditch, the Camry heading west at a thoughtful three miles an hour above the speed limit.

The motel Keller picked was an independent mom-and-pop operation in Tempe, which was another suburb of Phoenix. He counted out cash and paid a week in advance, plus a twenty-dollar deposit for phone calls. He didn't plan to make any calls, but if he needed to use the phone he wanted it to work.

He registered as David Miller of San Francisco, and fabricated an address and zip code. You were supposed to include your license plate number, and he mixed up a couple of digits and put CA for the state instead of AZ. It was hardly worth the trouble, nobody was going to look at the registration card, but there were certain things he did out of habit, and this was one of them.

He always traveled light, never took along more than a small carry-on bag with a shirt or two and a couple changes of socks and underwear. That made sense when you were flying, and less sense when you had a car with an empty trunk and back seat at your disposal. By the time he got to Phoenix, he'd run through his socks and underwear. He picked up two three-packs of briefs and a six-pack of socks at a strip mall, and was looking for a trash bin for his dirty clothes when he spotted a Goodwill Industries collection box. He felt good dropping his soiled socks and underwear in the box, though not quite as good as he'd felt dishing out designer food to the smoke-stained rescue workers at Ground Zero.

Back at his motel, he called Dot on the prepaid cell phone he'd picked up on 23rd Street. He'd paid cash for it, and hadn't even been asked his name, so as far as he could tell it was completely untraceable. At best someone could identify calls made from it as originating with a phone manufactured in Finland and sold at Radio Shack. Even if they managed to pin down the specific Radio Shack outlet, so what? There was nothing to tie it to Keller, or to Phoenix.

On the other hand, cell phone communications were about as secure as shouting. Any number of listening devices could pick up your conversation, and whatever you said was very likely being heard by half a dozen people on their car radios and one old fart who was catching every word on the fillings in his teeth. That didn't bother Keller, who figured every phone was tapped, and acted accordingly.

He phoned Dot, and the phone rang seven or eight times, and he broke the connection. She was probably out, he decided, or in the shower. Or had he misdialed? Always a chance, he thought, and pressed Redial, then caught himself and realized that, if he had in fact misdialed, redialing would just repeat the mistake. He broke the connection again in midring and punched in the number afresh, and this time he got a busy signal.

He tried it again, got another busy signal, frowned, waited, and tried again. It had barely begun to ring when she picked up, barking "Yes?" into the phone, and somehow fitting a full measure of irritation into the single syllable.

"It's me," he said.

"What a surprise."

"Is something wrong?"

"I had somebody at the door," she said, "and the teakettle was whistling, and I finally got to the phone and picked it up in time to listen to the dial tone."

"I let it ring a long time."

"That's nice. So I put it down and turned away, and it rang again, and I picked it up in the middle of the first ring, and I was just in time to hear you hang up."

He explained about pressing redial, and realizing that wouldn't work.

"Except it worked just fine," she said, "since you hadn't misdialed in the first place. I figured it had to be you, so I pressed star sixty-nine. But whatever phone you're on, star sixty-nine doesn't work. I got one of those weird tones and a canned message saying return calls to your number were blocked."

"It's a cell phone."

"Say no more. Hello? Where'd you go?"

"I'm here. You said *Say no more*, and . . ."

"It's an expression. Tell me it's all wrapped up and you're heading for home."

"I just got here."

"That's what I was afraid of. How's the weather?"

"Hot."

"Not here. They say it might snow, but then again it might not. You're just calling to check in, right?"

"Right."

"Well, it's good to hear your voice, and I'd love to chat, but you're on a cell phone."

"Right."

"Call anytime," she said. "It's always a treat to hear from you."

Keller didn't know the population or acreage of Sundowner Estates, although he had a hunch neither figure would be hard to come by. But what good would the information do him? The compound was large enough to contain a full-size eighteen-hole golf course, and enough homes adjacent to it to support the operation.

And there was a ten-foot adobe wall encircling the entire affair. Keller supposed it was easier to sell homes if you called it Sundowner Estates, but Fort Apache would have better conveyed the stockadelike feel of the place.

He drove around the compound a couple of times, establishing that there were in fact two gates, one at the east and the other not quite opposite, at the southwest corner. He parked where he could keep an eye on the southwest gate, and couldn't tell much beyond the fact that every vehicle entering or leaving the compound had to stop for some sort of exchange with the uniformed guard. Maybe you flashed a pass at him, maybe he called to make sure you were expected, maybe they wanted a thumbprint and a semen sample. No way to tell, not from where Keller was watching, but he was pretty sure he couldn't just drive up and bluff his way through. People who willingly lived behind a thick wall almost twice their own height probably expected a high level of security, and a guard who failed to provide that would be looking for a new job.

He drove back to his motel, sat in front of the TV and watched a special on the Discovery Channel about scuba diving at Australia's Great Barrier Reef. Keller didn't think it looked like something he wanted to do. He'd tried snorkeling once, on a vacation in Aruba, and kept having to stop because he was getting water in his snorkel, and under his mask. And he hadn't been able to see much of anything, anyhow.

The divers on the Discovery Channel were having much better luck, and there were plenty of colorful fish for them (and Keller) to look at. After fifteen minutes, though, he'd seen as much as he wanted to, and was ready to change the channel. It seemed like a lot of trouble to go through, flying all the way to Australia, then getting in the water with a mask and fins. Couldn't you get pretty much the same effect staring into a fish tank at a pet shop, or a Chinese restaurant?

"I'll tell you this," the woman said. "If you do make a decision to buy at Sundowner, you won't regret it. Nobody ever has."

"That's quite a recommendation," Keller said.

"Well, it's quite an operation, Mr. Miller. I don't suppose I have to ask if you play golf."

"It's somewhere between a pastime and an addiction," he said.

"I hope you brought your clubs. Sundowner's a championship course, you know. Robert Walker Wilson designed it, and Clay Bunis was a consultant. We're in the middle of the desert, but you wouldn't know it inside the walls at Sundowner. The course is as green as a pasture in the Irish midlands."

Her name, Keller learned, was Michelle Prentice, but everyone called her Mitzi. And what about him? Did he prefer Dave or David?

That was a stumper, and Keller realized he was taking too long to answer it. "It depends," he said, finally. "I answer to either one."

"I'll bet business associates call you Dave," she said, "and really close friends call you David."

"How on earth did you know that?"

She smiled broadly, delighted to be right. "Just a guess," she said. "Just a lucky guess, David."

So they were going to be close friends, he thought. Toward that end she proceeded to tell him a few things about herself, and by the time they reached the guard shack at the east gate of Sundowner Estates, he learned that she was thirty-nine years old, that she'd divorced her rat bastard of a husband three years ago and moved out here from Frankfort, Kentucky, which happened to be the state capital, although most people would guess it was Louisville. She'd sold houses in Frankfort, so she'd picked up an Arizona Realtor's license first chance she got, and it was a lot better selling houses here than it had ever been in Kentucky, because they just about sold themselves. The entire Phoenix area was growing like a house on fire, she assured him, and she was just plain excited to be a part of it all.

At the east gate she moved her sunglasses up onto her forehead and gave the guard a big smile. "Hi, Harry," she said. "Mitzi Prentice, and this here's Mr. Miller, come for a look at the Lattimore house on Saguaro Circle."

"Miz Prentice," he said, returning her smile and nodding at Keller. He consulted a clipboard, then slipped into the shack and picked up a telephone. After a moment he emerged and told Mitzi she could go ahead. "I guess you know how to get there," he said.

"I guess I ought to," she told Keller, after they'd driven away from the entrance. "I showed the house two days ago, and he was there to let me by. But he's got his job to do, and they take it seriously, let me tell you. I know not to joke with him, or with any of them, because they won't joke back. They can't, because it might not look good on camera."

"There are security cameras running?"

"Twenty-four hours a day. You don't get in unless your name's on the list, and the camera's got a record of when you came and went, and what car you were driving, license plate number and all."

"Really."

"There are some very affluent people at Sundowner," she said, "and some of them are getting along in years. That's not to say you won't find plenty of people your age here, especially on the golf course and around the pool, but you do get some older folks, too, and they tend to be a little more concerned about security. Now just look, David. Isn't that a beautiful sight?"

She pointed out her window at the golf course, and it looked like a golf course to him. He agreed it sure looked gorgeous.

The living room of the Lattimore house had a cathedral ceiling and a walk-in fireplace. Keller thought the fireplace looked nice, but he didn't quite get it. A walk-in closet was one thing, you could walk into it and pick what you wanted to wear, but why would anybody want to walk into a fireplace?

For that matter, who'd want to hold a prayer service in the living room?

He thought of raising the point with Mitzi. She might find either question provocative, but would it fit the Serious Buyer image he was trying to project? So he asked instead what he figured were more typical questions, about heating and cooling systems and financing, good basic home-buyer questions.

There was, predictably enough, a big picture window in the living room, and it afforded the predictable view of the golf course, overlooking what Mitzi told him were the fifth green and the sixth tee. There was a man taking practice swings who might have been W. W. Egmont himself, although from this distance and angle it was hard to say one way or the other. But if the guy turned a little to his left, and if Keller could look at him not with his naked eye but through a pair of binoculars—

Or, he thought, a telescopic sight. That would be quick and easy, wouldn't it? All he had to do was buy the place and set up in the living room with a high-powered rifle, and Egmont's state-of-the-art home burglar alarm wouldn't do him a bit of good. Keller could just perch there like a vulture, and sooner or later Egmont would finish up the fifth hole by four-putting for a triple bogey, and Keller could take him right there and save the poor duffer a stroke or wait until he came even closer and teed up his ball for the sixth hole (525 yards, par 5). Keller was no great shakes as a marksman, but how hard could it be to center the crosshairs on a target and squeeze the trigger?

"I bet you're picturing yourself on that golf course right now," Mitzi said, and he grinned and told her she got that one right.

———

From the bedroom window in the back of the house, you could look out at a desert garden, with cacti and succulents growing in sand. The plantings, like the bright green lawn in front, were all the responsibility of the Sundowners Estates association, who took care of all maintenance. They kept it beautiful year-round, she told him, and you never had to lift a finger.

"A lot of people think they want to garden when they retire," she said, "and then they find out how much work it can be. And what happens when you want to take off for a couple of weeks in Maui? At Sundowner, you can walk out the door and know everything's going to be beautiful when you come back."

He said he could see how that would be a comfort. "I can't see the fence from here," he said. "I was wondering about that, if you'd feel like you were walled in. I mean, it's nice looking, being adobe and earth-colored and all, but it's a pretty high fence."

"Close to twelve feet," she said.

Even higher than he'd thought. He said he wondered what it would be like living next to it, and she said none of the houses were close enough to the fence for it to be a factor.

"The design was very well thought out," she said. "There's the twelve-foot fence, and then there's a big space, anywhere from ten to twenty yards, and then there's an inner fence, also of adobe, that stands about five feet tall, and there's cactus and vines in front of it for landscaping, so it looks nice and decorative."

"That's a great idea," he said. And he liked it; all he had to do was clear the first fence and follow the stretch of no-man's-land around to wherever he felt like vaulting the shorter wall. "About the taller fence, though. I mean, it's not really terribly secure, is it?"

"What makes you say that?"

"Well, I don't know. I guess it's because I'm used to the Northeast, where security's pretty up front and obvious, but it's just a plain old mud fence, isn't it? No razor wire on top, no electrified fencing. It looks as though all a person would have to do is lean a long ladder up against it and he'd be over the top in a matter of seconds."

She laid a hand on his arm. "David," she said, "you asked that very casually, but I have the sense that security's a real concern of yours."

"I have a stamp collection," he said. "It's not worth a fortune, and collections are hard to sell, but the point is I've been collecting since I was a kid and I'd hate to lose it."

"I can understand that."

"So security's a consideration, yes. And the fellow at the gate's enough to put anybody's mind at rest, but if any jerk with a ladder can just pop right over the fence—"

It was, she told him, a little more complicated than that. There was no razor or concertina wire, because that made a place look like a concentration camp, but there were sensors that set up some kind of force field, and no one could begin to climb the fence without setting off all kinds of alarms. Nor were you home free once you cleared the fence, because there were dogs that patrolled the belt of no-man's-land, Dobermans, swift and silent.

"And there's an unmarked patrol car that circles the perimeter at regular intervals twenty-four hours a day," she said, "so if they spotted you on your way to the fence with a ladder under your arm—"

"It wouldn't be me," he assured her. "I like dogs okay, but I'd just as soon not meet those Dobermans you just mentioned."

It was, he decided, a good thing he'd asked. Earlier, he'd found a place to buy an aluminum extension ladder. He could have been over the fence in a matter of seconds, just in time to keep a date with Mr. Swift and Mr. Silent.

In the Lattimore kitchen, they sat across a table topped with butcher block and Mitzi went over the fine points with him. The furniture was all included, she told him, and as he could see it was in excellent condition. He might want to make some changes, of course, as a matter of personal taste, but the place was in turnkey condition. He could buy it today and move in tomorrow.

"In a manner of speaking," she said, and touched his arm again. "Financing takes a little time, and even if you were to pay cash it would take a few days to push the paperwork through. Were you thinking in terms of cash?"

"It's always simpler," he said.

"It is, but I'm sure you wouldn't have trouble with a mortgage. The banks love to write mortgages on Sundowner properties, because the prices only go up." Her fingers encircled his wrist. "I'm not sure I should tell you this, David, but now's a particularly good time to make an offer."

"Mr. Lattimore's eager to sell?"

"Mr. Lattimore couldn't care less," she said. "About selling or anything else. It's his daughter who'd like to sell. She had an offer of ten percent under the asking price, but she'd just listed the property and she turned it down, thinking the buyer'd boost it a little, but instead the buyer went and bought something else, and that woman's been kicking herself ever since. What *I* would do, I'd offer fifteen percent under what she's asking. You might not get it for that, but the worst you'd do is get it for ten percent under, and that's a bargain in this market."

He nodded thoughtfully, and asked what happened to Lattimore. "It was very sad," she said, "although in another sense it wasn't, because he died doing what he loved."

"Playing golf," Keller guessed.

"He hit a very nice tee shot on the thirteenth hole," she said, "which is a par four with a dogleg to the right. 'That's a sweet shot,' his partner said, and Mr. Lattimore said, 'Well, I guess I can still hit one now and then, can't I?' And then he just went and dropped dead."

"If you've got to go . . ."

"That's what everyone said, David. The body was cremated, and then they had a nice nondenominational service in the clubhouse, and afterward his daughter and son-in-law rode golf carts to the sixteenth hole and put his ashes in the water hazard." She laughed involuntarily, and let go of his wrist to cover her mouth with her hand. "Pardon me for laughing, but I was thinking what somebody said. How his balls were already there, and now he could go look for them."

Her hand returned to his wrist. He looked at her, and her eyes were looking back at him. "Well," he said. "My car's at your office, so you'd better run me back there. And then I'll want to get back to where I'm staying and freshen up, but after that I'd love to take you to dinner."

"Oh, I wish," she said.

"You have plans?"

"My daughter lives with me," she said, "and I like to be home with her on school nights, and especially tonight because there's a program on television we never miss."

"I see."

"So you're on your own for dinner," she said, "but what do you and I care about dinner, David? Why don't you just take me into old Mr. Lattimore's bedroom and fuck me senseless?"

She had a nice body and used it eagerly and imaginatively. Keller, his mind on his work, had been only vaguely aware of the sexual possibilities, and had in fact surprised himself by asking her to dinner. In the Lattimore bedroom he surprised himself further.

Afterward she said, "Well, I had high expectations, but I have to say they were exceeded. Isn't it a good thing I'm busy tonight? Otherwise it'd be a couple of hours before we even got to the restaurant, and ages before we got to bed. I mean, why waste all that time?"

He tried to think of something to say, but she didn't seem to require comment. "For all those years," she said, "I was the most faithful wife since Penelope. And it's not like nobody was interested. Men used to hit on me all the time. David, I even had girls hitting on me."

"Really."

"But I was never interested, and if I was, if I felt a little itch, a little tickle, well, I just pushed it away and put it out of my mind. Because of a little thing called marriage. I'd made some vows, and I took them seriously.

"And then I found out the son of a bitch was cheating on me, and it turned out it was nothing new. On our wedding day? It was years before I knew it, but that son of a bitch got lucky with one of my bridesmaids. And over the years he was catting around all the time. Not just my friends, but my sister."

"Your sister?"

"Well, my half-sister, really. My daddy died when I was little, and my mama remarried, and that's where she came from." She told him more than he needed to know about her childhood, and he lay there with his eyes closed and let the words wash over him. He hoped there wasn't going to be a test, because he wasn't paying close attention. . . .

"So I decided to make up for lost time," she said.

He'd dozed off, and after she woke him they'd showered in separate bathrooms. Now they were dressed again, and he'd followed her into the kitchen, where she opened the refrigerator and seemed surprised to find it empty.

She closed it and turned to him and said, "When I meet someone I feel like sleeping with, well, I go ahead and do it. I mean, why wait?"

"Works for me," he said.

"The only thing I don't like to do," she said, "is mix business and pleasure. So I made sure not to commit myself until I knew you weren't going to buy this place. And you're not, are you?"

"How did you know?"

"A feeling I got, when I said how you should make an offer. Instead of trying to think how much to offer, you were looking for a way out—or at least that was what I picked up. Which was okay with me, because by then I was more interested in getting laid than in selling a house. I didn't have to tell you about a whole lot of tax advantages, and how easy it is to rent the place out during the time you spend somewhere else. It's all pretty persuasive, and I could give you that whole rap now, but you don't really want to hear it, do you?"

"I might be in the market in a little while," he said, "but you're right, I'm nowhere near ready to make an offer at the present time. I suppose it was wrong of me to drag you out here and waste your time, but—"

"Do you hear me complaining, David?"

"Well, I just wanted to see the place," he said. "So I exaggerated my interest somewhat. Whether or not I'll be interested in settling in here depends on the outcome of a couple of business matters, and it'll be a while before I know how they're going to turn out."

"Sounds interesting," she said.

"I wish I could talk about it, but you know how it is."

"You could tell me," she said, "but then you'd have to kill me. In that case, don't you say a word."

He ate dinner by himself in a Mexican restaurant that reminded him of another Mexican restaurant. He was lingering over a second cup of café con leche before he figured it out. Years ago work had taken him to Roseburg, Oregon, and before he got out of there he'd picked out a real estate agent and spent an afternoon driving around looking at houses for sale.

He hadn't gone to bed with the Oregon realtor, or even considered it, nor had he used her as a way to get information on an approach to his quarry. That man, whom the Witness Protection Program had imperfectly protected, had been all too easy to find, but Keller, who ordinarily knew well enough to keep his business and personal life separate, had somehow let himself befriend the poor bastard. Before he knew it he was having fantasies about moving to Roseburg himself, buying a house, getting a dog, settling down.

He'd looked at houses, but that was as far as he'd let it go. The night came when he got a grip on himself, and the next thing he got a grip on was the man who'd brought him there. He used a garrote, and what he got a grip on was on the guy's throat, and then it was time to go back to New York.

He remembered the Mexican café in Roseburg now. The food had been good, though he didn't suppose it was all that special, and he'd had a mild crush on the waitress, about as realistic as the whole idea of moving there. He thought of the man he'd killed, an accountant who'd become the proprietor of a quick-print shop.

You could learn the business in a couple of hours, the man had said of his new career. *You could buy the place and move in the same day*, Mitzi had said of the Lattimore house.

Patterns . . .

You could tell me, she'd said, thinking she was joking, *but then you'd have to kill me*. Oddly, in the languor that followed their lovemaking, he'd had the impulse to confide in her, to tell her what had brought him to Scottsdale.

Yeah, right.

He drove around for a while, then found his way back to his motel and surfed the TV channels without finding anything that caught his interest. He turned off the set and sat there in the dark.

He thought of calling Dot. There were things he could talk about with her, but others he couldn't, and anyway he didn't want to do any talking on a cell phone, not even an untraceable one.

He found himself thinking about the guy in Roseburg. He tried to picture him and couldn't. Early on he'd worked out a way to keep people from the past from flooding the present with their faces. You worked with their images in your mind, leached the color out of them, made the features grow dimmer, shrank the picture as if viewing it through the wrong end of a telescope. You made them grow smaller and darker and hazier until they disappeared, and if you did it correctly you forgot everything but the barest of facts about them. There was no emotional charge, no weight to them, and they became more and more difficult to recall to mind.

But now he'd bridged a gap and closed a circuit, and the man's face was there in his memory, the face of an aging chipmunk. Jesus, Keller thought, get out of my memory, will you? You've been dead for years. Leave me the hell alone.

If you were here, he told the face, I could talk to you. And you'd listen, because what the hell else could you do? You couldn't talk back, you couldn't judge me, you couldn't tell me to shut up. You're dead, so you couldn't say a goddam word.

He went outside, walked around for a while, came back in and sat on the edge of the bed. Very deliberately he set about getting rid of the man's face, washing it of color, pushing it farther and farther away, making it disappear. The process was more difficult than it had been in years, but it worked, finally, and the little man was gone to wherever the washed-out faces of dead people went. Wherever it was, Keller prayed he'd stay there.

He took a long hot shower and went to bed.

In the morning he found someplace new to have breakfast. He read the paper and had a second cup of coffee, then drove pointlessly around the perimeter of Sundowner Estates.

Back at the motel, he called Dot on his cell phone. "Here's what I've been able to come up with," he said. "I park where I can watch the entrance. Then, when some resident drives out, I follow them."

"Them?"

"Well, him or her, depending which it is. Or them, if there's more than one in the car. Sooner or later, they stop somewhere and get out of the car."

"And you take them out, and you keep doing this, and sooner or later it's the right guy."

"They get out of the car," he said, "and I hang around until nobody's watching, and I get in the trunk."

"The trunk of their car."

"If I wanted to get in the trunk of my own car," he said, "I could go do that right now. Yes, the trunk of their car."

"I get it," she said. "Their car morphs into the Trojan Chrysler. They sail back into the walled city, and you're in there, and hoping they'll open the trunk eventually and let you out."

"Car trunks have a release mechanism built in these days," he said. "So kidnap victims can escape."

"You're kidding," she said. "The auto makers added something for the benefit of the eight people a year who get stuffed into car trunks?"

"I think it's probably more than eight a year," he said, "and then there are the people, kids mostly, who get locked in accidentally. Anyway, it's no problem getting out."

"How about getting in? You real clever with auto locks?"

"That might be a problem," he admitted. "Does everybody lock their car nowadays?"

"I bet the ones who live in gated communities do. Not when they're home safe, but when they're out and about in a dangerous place like the suburbs of Phoenix. How crazy are you about this plan, Keller?"

"Not too," he admitted.

"Because how would you even know they were going back? Your luck, they're on their way to spend two weeks in Las Vegas."

"I didn't think of that."

"Of course you'd know right away," she said, "when you tried to get in the trunk and it was full of suitcases and copies of *Beat the Dealer*."

"It's not a great plan," he allowed, "but you wouldn't believe the security. The only other thing I can think of is to buy a place."

"Buy a house there, you mean. I don't think the budget would cover it."

"I could keep it as an investment," he said, "and rent it out when I wasn't using it."

"Which would be what, fifty-two weeks a year?"

"But if I could afford to do all that," he said, "I could also afford to tell the client to go roll his hoop, which I'm thinking I might have to go and do anyway."

"Because it's looking difficult."

"It's looking impossible," he said, "and then on top of everything else . . ."

"Yes? Keller? Where'd you go? Hello?"

"Never mind," he said. "I just figured out how to do it."

"As you can see," Mitzi Prentice said, "the view's nowhere near as
nice as the Lattimore house. And there's just two bedrooms instead
of three, and the furnishing's a little on the generic side. But compared to spending the next two weeks in a motel—"

"It's a whole lot more comfortable," he said.

"And more secure," she said, "just in case you've got your stamp
collection with you."

"I don't," he said, "but a little security never hurt anybody. I'd
like to take it."

"I don't blame you, it's a real good deal, and nice income for Mr.
and Mrs. Sundstrom, who're in the Galapagos Islands looking at
blue-footed boobies. That's where all the crap on their walls comes
from. Not the Galapagos, but other places they go to on their travels."

"I was wondering."

"Well, they could tell you about each precious piece, but they're
not here, and if they were then their place wouldn't be available,
would it? We'll go to the office and fill out the paperwork, and then
you can give me a check and I'll give you a set of keys and some ID
to get you past the guard at the gate. And a pass to the clubhouse,
and information on greens fees and all. I hope you'll have some time
for golf."

"Oh, I should be able to fit in a few rounds."

"No telling what you'll be able to fit in," she said. "Speaking of
which, let's fit in a quick stop at the Lattimore house before we start
filling out lease agreements. And no, silly, I'm not trying to get you to
buy that place. I just want you to take me into that bedroom again. I
mean, you don't expect me to do it in Cynthia Sundstrom's bed, do
you? With all those weird masks on the wall? It'd give me the jimjams for sure. I'd feel like primitive tribes were watching me."

The Sundstrom house was a good deal more comfortable than his
motel, and he found he didn't mind being surrounded by souvenirs

of the couple's travels. The second bedroom, which evidently served as Harvey Sundstrom's den, had a collection of edged weapons hanging on the walls, knives and daggers and what he supposed were battle-axes, and there was no end of carved masks and tapestries in the other rooms. Some of the masks looked godawful, he supposed, but they weren't the sort of things to give him the jimjams, whatever the jimjams might be, and he got in the habit of acknowledging one of them, a West African mask with teeth like tombstones and a lot of rope fringe for hair. He found himself giving it a nod when he passed it, even raising a hand in a salute.

Pretty soon, he thought, he'd be talking to it.

Because it was becoming clear to him that he felt the need to talk to someone. It was, he supposed, a need he'd had all his life, but for years he'd led an existence that didn't much lend itself to sharing confidences. He'd spent virtually all his adult life as a paid assassin, and it was no line of work for a man given to telling his business to strangers—or to friends, for that matter. You did what they paid you to do and you kept your mouth shut, and that was about it. You didn't talk about your work, and it got so you didn't talk about much of anything else, either. You could go to a sports bar and talk about the game with the fellow on the next barstool, you could gripe about the weather to the woman standing alongside you at the bus stop, you could complain about the mayor to the waitress at the corner coffee shop, but if you wanted a conversation with a little more substance to it, well, you were pretty much out of luck.

Once, a few years ago, he'd let someone talk him into going to a psychotherapist. He'd taken what struck him as reasonable precautions, paying cash, furnishing a false name and address, and essentially limiting disclosures to his childhood. It was productive, too, and he developed some useful insights, but in the end it went bad, with the therapist drawing some unwelcome inferences and eventually following Keller, and learning things he wasn't supposed to know about him. The man wanted to become a client himself, and of course Keller couldn't allow that, and made him a quarry instead. So much for therapy. So much for shared confidences.

Then, for some months after the therapist's exit, he'd had a dog. Not Soldier, the dog of his boyhood years, but Nelson, a fine Australian cattle dog. Nelson had turned out to be not only the perfect companion but the perfect confidante. You could tell him anything, secure in the knowledge that he'd keep it to himself, and it wasn't like talking to yourself or talking to the wall, because the dog was real and alive and gave every indication of paying close attention. There were times when he could swear Nelson understood every word.

He wasn't judgmental, either. You could tell him anything and he didn't love you any the less for it.

If only it had stayed that way, he thought. But it hadn't, and he supposed it was his own fault. He'd found someone to take care of Nelson when work took him out of town, and that was better than putting him in a kennel, but then he wound up falling for the dog walker, and she moved in, and he only really got to talk to Nelson when Andria was somewhere else. That wasn't too bad, and she was fun to have around, but then one day it was time for her to move on, and on she moved. He'd bought her no end of earrings during their time together, and she took the earrings along with her when she left, which was okay. But she also took Nelson, and there he was, right back where he started.

Another man might have gone right out and got himself another dog—and then, like as not, gone looking for a woman to walk it for him. Keller figured enough was enough. He hadn't replaced the therapist, and he hadn't replaced the dog, and, although women drifted in and out of his life, he hadn't replaced the girlfriend. He had, after all, lived alone for years, and it worked for him.

Most of the time, anyway.

"Now this is nice," Keller said. "The suburbs go on for a ways, but once you get past them you're out in the desert, and as long as you stay off the Interstate you've pretty much got the whole place to yourself. It's pleasant, isn't it?"

There was no answer from the passenger seat.

"I paid cash for the Sundstrom house," he went on. "Two weeks, a thousand dollars a week. That's more than a motel, but I can cook my own meals and save on restaurant charges. Except I like to go out for my meals. But I didn't drag you all the way out here to listen to me talk about stuff like that."

Again, his passenger made no response, but then he hadn't expected one.

"There's a lot I have to figure out," he said. "Like what I'm going to do with the rest of my life, for starters. I don't see how I can keep on doing what I've been doing all these years. If you think of it as killing people, taking lives, well, how could a person go on doing it year after year after year?

"But the thing is, see, you don't have to dwell on that aspect of the work. I mean, face it, that's what it is. These people are walking around, doing what they do, and then I come along, and whatever it is they've been doing, they don't get to do it anymore. Because they're dead, because I killed them."

He glanced over, looking for a reaction. Yeah, right.

"What happens," he said, "is you wind up thinking of each subject not as a person to be killed but as a problem to be solved. Here's this piece of work you have to do, and how do you get it done? How do you carry out the contract as expediently as possible, with the least stress all around?

"Now there are guys doing this," he went on, "who cope with it by making it personal. They find a reason to hate the guy they have to kill. They're mad at him, they're angry with him, because it's his fault that they've got to do this bad thing. If it weren't for him, they wouldn't be committing this sin. He's going to be the cause of them going to hell, the son of a bitch, so of course they're mad at him, of course they hate him, and that makes it easier for them to kill him, which is what they made up their minds to do in the first place.

"But that always struck me as silly. I don't know what's a sin and what isn't, or if one person deserves to go on living and another deserves to have his life ended. Sometimes I think about stuff like that, but as far as working it all out in my mind, well, I never seem to get anywhere.

"I could go on like this, but the thing is I'm okay with the moral aspects of it, if you want to call it that. I just think I'm getting a little old to be still at it, that's part of it, and the other's that the business has changed. It's the same in that there are still people who are willing to pay to have other people killed. You never have to worry about running out of clients. Sometimes business drops off for a while, but it always comes back again. Whether it's a guy like that Cuban in Miami, who must have had a hundred guys with a reason to want him dead, or this Egmont with his pot belly and his golf clubs, who you'd think would be unlikely to inspire strong feelings in anybody. All kinds of subjects, and all kinds of clients, and you never run out of either one."

The road curved, and he took the curve a little too fast, and had to reach over with his right hand to reposition his silent companion.

"You should be wearing your seat belt," he said. "Where was I? Oh, the way the business is changing. It's the world, really. Airport security, having to show ID everywhere you go. And gated communities, and all the rest of it. You think of Daniel Boone, who knew it was time to head west when he couldn't cut down a tree without giving some thought to which direction it was going to fall.

"I don't know, it seems to me that I'm just running off at the mouth, not making any sense. Well, that's okay. What do you care? Just so long as I take it easy on the curves so you don't wind up on the floor, you'll be perfectly willing to sit there and listen as long as I want to talk. Won't you?"

No response.

"If I played golf," he said, "I'd be out on the course every day, and I wouldn't have to burn up a tankful of gas driving around the desert. I'd spend all my time within the Sundowner walls, and I wouldn't have been walking around the mall, wouldn't have seen you in the display next to the cash register. A batch of different breeds on sale, and I'm not sure what you're supposed to be, but I guess you're some kind of terrier. They're good dogs, terriers. Feisty, lots of personality.

"I used to have an Australian cattle dog. I called him Nelson. Well, that was his name before I got him, and I didn't see any reason to change it. I don't think I'll give you a name. I mean, it's nutty enough, buying a stuffed animal, taking it for a ride and having a conversation with it. It's not as if you're going to answer to a name, or as if I'll relate to you on a deeper level if I hang a name on you. I mean, I may be crazy but I'm not stupid. I realize I'm talking to polyester and foam rubber, or whatever the hell you're made out of. Made in China, it says on the tag. That's another thing, everything's made in China or Indonesia or the Philippines, nothing's made in America anymore. It's not that I'm paranoid about it, it's not that I'm worried about all the jobs going overseas. What do I care, anyway? It's not affecting my work. As far as I know, nobody's flying in hired killers from Thailand and Korea to take jobs away from good home-grown American hit men.

"It's just that you have to wonder what people in this country are doing. If they're not making anything, if everything's imported from someplace else, what the hell do Americans do when they get to the office?"

He talked for a while more, then drove around some in silence, then resumed the one-sided conversation. Eventually he found his way back to Sundowner Estates, circling the compound and entering by the southwestern gate.

Hi, Mr. Miller. Hello, Harry. Hey, whatcha got there? Cute little fella, isn't he? A present for my sister's little girl, my niece. I'll ship it to her tomorrow.

The hell with that. Before he got to the guard shack, he reached into the back seat for a newspaper and spread it over the stuffed dog in the passenger seat.

In the clubhouse bar, Keller listened sympathetically as a fellow named Al went over his round of golf, stroke by stroke. "What kills me," Al said, "is that I just can't put it all together. Like on the seventh hole this afternoon, my drive's smack down the middle of the fairway, and my second shot with a three-iron is hole-high and just off the edge of the green on the right. I'm not in the bunker, I'm past it, and I've got a good lie maybe ten, twelve feet from the edge of the green."

"Nice," Keller said, his voice carefully neutral. If it wasn't nice, Al could assume he was being ironic.

"Very nice," Al agreed, "and I'm lying two, and all I have to do is run it up reasonably close and sink the putt for a par. I could use a wedge, but why screw around? It's easier to take this little chipping iron I carry and run it up close."

"Uh-huh."

"So I run it up close, all right, and it doesn't miss the cup by more than two inches, but I played it too strong, and it picks up speed and rolls past the pin and all the way off the green, and I wind up farther from the cup than when I started."

"Hell of a thing."

"So I chip again, and pass the hole again, though not quite as badly. And by the time I'm done hacking away with my goddam putter I'm three strokes over par with a seven. Takes me two strokes to cover four hundred and forty yards and five more strokes to manage the last fifty feet."

"Well, that's golf," Keller said.

"By God, you said a mouthful," Al said. "That's golf, all right.

How about another round of these, Dave, and then we'll get ourselves some dinner? There's a couple of guys you ought to meet."

He wound up at a table with four other fellows. Al and a man named Felix were residents of Sundowner Estates, while the other two men were Felix's guests, seasonal residents of Scottsdale who belonged to one of the other local country clubs. Felix told a long joke, involving a hapless golfer driven to suicide by a bad round of golf. For the punch line, Felix held his wrists together and said, "What time?" and everybody roared. They all ordered steaks and drank beer and talked about golf and politics and how screwed-up the stock market was these days, and Keller managed to keep up his end of the conversation without anybody seeming to notice that he didn't know what the hell he was talking about.

"So how'd you do out there today?" someone asked him, and Keller had his reply all ready.

"You know," he said thoughtfully, "it's a hell of a thing. You can hack away like a man trying to beat a ball to death with a stick, and then you hit one shot that's so sweet and true that it makes you feel good about the whole day."

He couldn't even remember when or where he'd heard that, but it evidently rang true with his dinner companions. They all nodded solemnly, and then someone changed the subject and said something disparaging about Democrats, and it was Keller's turn to nod in agreement.

Nothing to it.

"So we'll go out tomorrow morning," Al said to Felix. "Dave, if you want to join us . . ."

Keller pressed his wrists together, said, "What time?" When the laughter died down he said, "I wish I could, Al. I'm afraid tomorrow's out. Another time, though."

"You could take a lesson," Dot said. "Isn't there a club pro? Doesn't he give lessons?"

"There is," he said, "and I suppose he does, but why would I want to take one?"

"So you could get out there and play golf. Protective coloration and all."

"If anyone sees me swinging a golf club," he said, "with or without a lesson, they'll wonder what the hell I'm doing here. But this way they just figure I fit in a round earlier in the day. Anyway, I don't want to spend too much time around the clubhouse. Mostly I get the hell out of here and go for drives."

"On the driving range?"

"Out in the desert," she said.

"You just ride around and look at the cactus."

"There's a lot of it to look at," he said, "although they have a problem with poachers."

"You're kidding."

"No," he said, and explained how the cacti were protected, but criminals dug them up and sold them to florists.

"Cactus rustlers," Dot said. "That's the damnedest thing I ever heard of. I guess they have to be careful of the spines."

"I suppose so."

"Serve them right if they get stuck. You just drive around, huh?"

"And think things out."

"Well, that's nice. But you don't want to lose sight of the reason you moved in there in the first place."

He stayed away from the clubhouse the next day, and the day after. Then, on a Tuesday afternoon, he got in his car and drove around, staying within the friendly confines of Sundowner. He passed the Lattimore house and wondered if Mitzi Prentice had shown it to anyone lately. He drove past William Egmont's house, which looked to be pretty much the same model as the Sundstrom place. Egmont's Cadillac was parked in the carport, but the man owned his own golf cart, and Keller couldn't see it there. He'd probably motored over to the first tee on his cart, and might be out there now, taking big divots, slicing balls deep into the rough.

Keller went home, parked his Toyota in the Sundstrom carport. He'd worried, after taking the house for two weeks, that Mitzi would call all the time, or, worse, start turning up without calling first. But in fact he hadn't heard a word from her, for which he'd been deeply grateful, and now he found himself thinking about calling her, at work or at home, and figuring out a place to meet. Not at his place, because of the masks, and not at her place, because of her daughter, and—

That settled it. If he was starting to think like that, well, it was time he got on with it. Or the next thing you knew he'd be taking golf lessons, and buying the Lattimore house, and trading in the stuffed dog on a real one.

He went outside. The afternoon had already begun fading into early evening, and it seemed to Keller that the darkness came quicker here than it did in New York. That stood to reason, it was a good deal closer to the equator, and that would account for it. Someone had explained why to him once, and he'd understood it at the time, but now all that remained was the fact: the farther you were from the equator, the more extended twilight became.

In any event, the golfers were through for the day. He took a walk along the edge of the golf course, and passed Egmont's house. The car was still there, and the golf cart was not. He walked on for a while, then turned around and headed toward the house again, coming from the other direction, and saw someone gliding along on a motorized golf cart. Was it Egmont, on his way home? No, as the cart came closer he saw that the rider was thinner than Keller's quarry, and had a fuller head of hair. And the cart turned off before it reached Egmont's house, which pretty much cinched things.

Besides, he was soon to discover, Egmont had already returned. His cart was parked in the carport, alongside his car, and the bag of golf clubs was slung over the back of the cart. Something about that last touch reminded Keller of a song, though he couldn't pin down the song or figure out how it hooked up to the golf cart. Something mournful, something with bagpipes, but Keller couldn't put his finger on it.

There were lights on in Egmont's house. Was he alone? Had he brought someone home with him?

One easy way to find out. He walked up the path to the front door, poked the doorbell. He heard it ring, then didn't hear anything and considered ringing it again. First he tried the door, and found it locked, which was no great surprise, and then he heard footsteps, but just barely, as if someone was walking lightly on deep carpet. And then the door opened a few inches until the chain stopped it, and

William Wallis Egmont looked out at him, a puzzled expression on his face.

"Mr. Egmont?"

"Yes?"

"My name's Miller," he said. "David Miller. I'm staying just over the hill, I'm renting the Sundstrom house for a couple of weeks . . ."

"Oh, of course," Egmont said, visibly relaxing. "Of course, Mr. Miller. Someone was mentioning you just the other day. And I do believe I've seen you around the club. And out on the course, if I'm not mistaken."

It was a mistake Keller saw no need to correct. "You probably have," he said. "I'm out there every chance I get."

"As am I, sir. I played today and I expect to play tomorrow."

Keller pressed his wrists together, said, "What time?"

"Oh, very good," Egmont said. " 'What time?' That's a golfer for you, isn't it? Now how can I help you?"

"It's delicate," Keller said. "Do you suppose I could come in for a moment?"

"Well, I don't see why not," Egmont said, and slipped the chain lock to let him in.

The keypad for the burglar alarm was mounted on the wall, just to the right of the front door. Immediately adjacent to it was a sheet of paper headed HOW TO SET THE BURGLAR ALARM with the instructions hand-printed in block capitals large enough to be read easily by elderly eyes. Keller read the directions, followed them, and let himself out of Egmont's house. A few minutes later he was back in his own house—the Sundstrom house. He made himself a cup of coffee in the Sundstrom kitchen and sat with it in the Sundstrom living room, and while it cooled he let himself remember the last moments of William Wallis Egmont.

He practiced the exercises that were automatic for him by now, turning the images that came to mind from color to black and white, then watching them fade to gray, willing them farther and farther away so that they grew smaller and smaller until they were vanishing pinpoints, gray dots on a gray field, disappearing into the distance, swallowed up by the past.

When his coffee cup was empty he went into the Sundstrom bedroom and undressed, then showered in the Sundstrom bathroom, only to dry off with a Sundstrom towel. He went into the den, Harvey Sundstrom's den, and took a Fijian battle-axe from the wall. It was fashioned of black wood, and heavier than it looked, and its elaborate geometric shape suggested it would be of more use as wall decoration than weapon. But Keller worked out how to grip it and swing it, and took a few experimental whiffs with it, and he could see how the islanders would have found it useful.

He could have taken it with him to Egmont's house, and he let himself imagine it now, saw himself clutching the device in both hands and swinging around in a 360-degree arc, whipping the business end of the axe into Egmont's skull. He shook his head, returned the battle-axe to the wall, and resumed where he'd left off earlier, summoning up Egmont's image, reviewing the last moments of Egmont's life, and making it all gray and blurry, making it all smaller and smaller, making it all go away.

In the morning he went out for breakfast, returning in time to see an ambulance leaving Sundowner Estates through the east gate. The guard recognized Keller and waved him through, but he braked and rolled down the window to inquire about the ambulance. The guard shook his head soberly and reported the sad news.

He went home and called Dot. "Don't tell me," she said. "You've decided you can't do it."

"It's done."

"It's amazing how I can just sense these things," she said. "You figure it's psychic powers or old-fashioned feminine intuition? That was a rhetorical question, Keller. You don't have to answer it. I'd say I'll see you tomorrow, but I won't, will I?"

"It'll take me a while to get home."

"Well, no rush," she said. "Take your time, see the sights. You've got your clubs, haven't you?"

"My clubs?"

"Stop along the way, play a little golf. Enjoy yourself, Keller. You deserve it."

The day before his two-week rental was up, he walked over to the clubhouse, settled his account, and turned in his keys and ID card. He walked back to the Sundstrom house, where he put his suitcase in the trunk and the little stuffed dog in the passenger seat. Then he got behind the wheel and drove slowly around the golf course, leaving the compound by the east gate.

"It's a nice place," he told the dog. "I can see why people like it. Not just the golf and the weather and the security. You get the feeling nothing really bad could happen to you there. Even if you die, it's just part of the natural order of things."

He set cruise control and pointed the car toward Tucson, lowering the visor against the morning sun. It was, he thought, good weather for cruise control. Just the other day, he'd had NPR on the car radio, and listened as a man with a professionally mellow voice cautioned against using cruise control in wet weather. If the car were to hydroplane on the slick pavement, cruise control would think the wheels weren't turning fast enough, and would speed up the engine to compensate. And then, when the tires got their grip again, wham!

Keller couldn't recall the annual cost in lives from this phenomenon, but it was higher than you'd think. At the time all he did was resolve to make sure he took the car out of cruise control whenever he switched on the windshield wipers. Now, cruising east across the Arizona desert, he found himself wondering if there might be any practical application for this new knowledge. Accidental death was a useful tool, it had most recently claimed the life of William Wallis Egmont, but Keller couldn't see how cruise control in inclement weather could become part of his bag of tricks. Still, you never knew, and he let himself think about it.

In Tucson he stuck the dog in his suitcase before he turned in the car, then walked out into the heat and managed to locate his original car in long-term parking. He tossed his suitcase in the back seat and stuck the key in the ignition, wondering if the car would start. No problem if it wouldn't, all he'd have to do was talk to somebody at the Hertz counter, but suppose they'd just noticed him at the Avis counter, turning in another car. Would they notice something like that? You wouldn't think so, but airports were different these days. There were people standing around noticing everything.

He turned the key, and the engine turned over right away. The woman at the gate figured out what he owed and sounded apologetic when she named the figure. He found himself imagining what the charges would have added up to on other cars he'd left in long-term lots, cars he'd never returned to claim, cars with bodies in their trunks. Probably a lot of money, he decided, and nobody to pay it. He figured he could afford to pick up the tab for a change. He paid cash, took the receipt, and got back on the Interstate.

As he drove, he found himself figuring out just how he'd have handled it if the car hadn't started. "For God's sake," he said, "look at yourself, will you? Something could have happened but didn't, it's over and done with, and you're figuring out what you would have done, developing a coping strategy when there's nothing to cope with. What the hell's the matter with you?"

He thought about it. Then he said, "You want to know what's the matter with you? You're talking to yourself, that's what's the matter with you."

He stopped doing it. Twenty minutes down the road he pulled into a rest area, leaned over the seat back, opened his suitcase, and returned the dog to its position in the passenger seat.

"And away we go," he said.

In New Mexico he got off the Interstate and followed the signs to an Indian pueblo. A plump woman, her hair braided and her face expressionless, sat in a room with pots she had made herself. Keller picked out a little black pot with scalloped edges. She wrapped it carefully for him, using sheets of newspaper, and put the wrapped pot in a brown paper bag, and the paper bag into a plastic bag. Keller tucked the whole thing away in his suitcase and got back behind the wheel.

"Don't ask," he told the dog.

Just over the Colorado state line it started to rain. He drove through the rain for ten or twenty miles before he remembered the guy on NPR. He tapped the brake, which made the cruise control cut out, but just to make sure he used the switch, too.

"Close one," he told the dog.

In Kansas he took a state road north and visited a roadside attraction, a house that had once been a hideout of the Dalton boys. They were outlaws, he knew, contemporaries of the Jesse James and the Youngers. The place was tricked out as a mini museum, with memorabilia and news clippings, and there was an underground passage leading from the house to the barn in back, so that the brothers, when surprised by the law, could hurry through the tunnel and escape that way. He'd have liked to see the passage, but it was sealed off.

"Still," he told the woman attendant, "it's nice to know it's there."

If he was interested in the Daltons, she told him, there was another museum at the other end of the state. At Coffeyville, she said, where as he probably knew most of the Daltons were killed, trying to rob two banks in one day. He had in fact known that, but only because he'd just read it on the information card for one of the exhibits.

He stopped at a gas station, bought a state map, and figured out the route to Coffeyville. Halfway there he stopped for the night at a Red Roof Inn, had a pizza delivered, and ate it in front of the television set. He ran the cable channels until he found a western that looked promising, and damned if it didn't turn out to be about the Dalton boys. Not just the Daltons—Frank and Jesse James were in it, too, and Cole Younger and his brothers.

They seemed like real nice fellows, too, the kind of guys you wouldn't mind hanging out with. Not a sadist or pyromaniac in the lot, as far as he could tell. And did you think Jesse James wet the bed? Like hell he did.

In the morning he drove on to Coffeyville and paid the admission charge and took his time studying the exhibits. It was a pretty bold act, robbing two banks at once, but it might not have been the smartest move in the history of American crime. The local citizens were just waiting for them, and they riddled the brothers with bullets. Most of them were dead by the time the shooting stopped, or died of their wounds before long.

Emmett Dalton wound up with something like a dozen bullets in him, and went off to prison. But the story didn't end there. He recovered, and eventually got released, and wound up in Los Angeles, where he wrote films for the young motion picture industry and made a small fortune in real estate.

Keller spent a long time taking that in, and it gave him a lot to think about.

Most of the time he was quiet, but now and then he talked to the dog.

"Take soldiers," he said, on a stretch of 1-40 east of Des Moines. "They get drafted into the army, they go through basic training, and before you know it they're aiming at other soldiers and pulling the trigger. Maybe they have to force themselves the first couple of times, and maybe they have bad dreams early on, but then they get used to it, and before you know it they sort of enjoy it. It's not a sex thing, they don't get that kind of a thrill out of it, but it's sort of like hunting. Except you just pull the trigger and leave it at that. You don't have to track wounded soldiers to make sure they don't suffer. You don't have to dress your kill and pack it back to camp. You just pull the trigger and get on with your life.

"And these are ordinary kids," he went on. "Eighteen-year-old boys, drafted fresh out of high school. Or I guess it's volunteers now, they don't draft them anymore, but it amounts to the same thing. They're just ordinary American boys. They didn't grow up torturing animals or starting fires. Or wetting the bed.

"You know something? I still don't see what wetting the bed has to do with it."

Coming into New York on the George Washington Bridge, he said, "Well, they're not there."

The towers, he meant. And of course they weren't there, they were gone, and he knew that. He'd been down to the site enough times to know it wasn't trick photography, that the twin towers were in fact gone. But somehow he'd half expected to see them, half expected the whole thing to turn out to have been a dream. You couldn't make part of the skyline disappear, for God's sake.

He drove to the Hertz place, returned the car. He was walking away from the office with his suitcase in hand when an attendant rushed up, brandishing the little stuffed dog. "You forgot somethin'," the man said, smiling broadly.

"Oh, right," Keller said. "You got any kids?"

"Me?"

"Give it to your kid," Keller told him. "Or some other kid."

"You don't want him?"

He shook his head, kept walking. When he got home he showered and shaved and looked out the window. His window faced east, not south, and had never afforded a view of the towers, so it was the same as it had always been. And that's why he'd looked, to assure himself that everything was still there, that nothing had been taken away.

It looked okay to him. He picked up the phone and called Dot.

She was waiting for him on the porch, with the usual pitcher of iced tea. "You had me going," she said. "You didn't call and you didn't call and you didn't call. It took you the better part of a month to get home. What did you do, walk?"

"I didn't leave right away," he said. "I paid for two weeks."

"And you wanted to make sure you got your money's worth."

"I thought it'd be suspicious, leaving early. 'Oh, I remember that guy, he left four days early, right after Mr. Egmont died.'"

"And you thought it'd be safer to hang around the scene of a homicide?"

"Except it wasn't a homicide," he said. "The man came home after an afternoon at the golf course, locked his door, set the burglar alarm, got undressed and drew a hot bath. He got into the tub and lost consciousness and drowned."

"Most accidents happen in the home," Dot said. "Isn't that what they say? What did he do, hit his head?"

"He may have smacked it on the tile on the way down, after he lost his balance. Or maybe he had a little stroke. Hard to say."

"You undressed him and everything?"

He nodded. "Put him in the tub. He came to in the water, but I picked up his feet and held them in the air, and his head went under, and, well, that was that."

"Water in the lungs."

"Right."

"Death by drowning."

He nodded.

"You okay, Keller?"

"Me? Sure, I'm fine. Anyway, I figured I'd wait the four days, leave when my time was up."

"Just like Egmont."

"Huh?"

"He left when his time was up," she said. "Still, how long does it take to drive home from Phoenix? Four, five days?"

"I got sidetracked," he said, and told her about the Dalton boys.

"Two museums," she said. "Most people have never been to one Dalton boys museum, and you've been to two."

"Well, they robbed two banks at once."

"What's that got to do with it?"

"I don't know. Nothing, I guess. You ever hear of Nashville, Indiana?"

"I've heard of Nashville," she said, "and I've heard of Indiana, but I guess the answer to your questions is no. What have they got in Nashville, Indiana? The Grand Ole Hoosier Opry?"

"There's a John Dillinger museum there."

"Jesus, Keller. What were you taking, an outlaw's tour of the Midwest?"

"There was a flyer for the place in the museum in Coffeyville, and it wasn't that far out of my way. It was interesting. They had the fake gun he used to break out of prison. Or it may have been a replica. Either way, it was pretty interesting."

"I'll bet."

"They were folk heroes," he said. "Dillinger and Pretty Boy Floyd and Baby Face Nelson."

"And Bonnie and Clyde. Have those two got a museum?"

"Probably. They were heroes the same as the Daltons and Youngers and Jameses, but they weren't brothers. Back in the nineteenth century it was a family thing, but then that tradition died out."

"Kids today," Dot said. "What about Ma Barker? Wasn't that around the same time as Dillinger? And didn't she have a whole houseful of bank-robbing brats? Or was that just in the movies?"

"No, you're right," he said. "I forgot about Ma Barker."

"Well, let's forget her all over again, so you can get to the point."

He shook his head. "I'm not sure there is one. I just took my time getting back, that's all. I had some thinking to do."

"And?"

He reached for the pitcher, poured himself more iced tea. "Okay," he said. "Here's the thing. I can't do this anymore."

"I can't say I'm surprised."

"I was going to retire a while ago," he said. "Remember?"

"Vividly."

"At the time," he said, "I figured I could afford it. I had money put aside. Not a ton, but enough for a little bungalow somewhere in Florida."

"And you could get to Denny's in time for the early bird special, which helps keep food costs down."

"You said I needed a hobby, and that got me interested in stamp collecting again. And before I knew it I was spending serious money on stamps."

"And that was the end of your retirement fund."

"It cut into it," he agreed. "And it's kept me from saving money ever since then, because any extra money just goes into stamps."

She frowned. "I think I see where this is going," she said. "You can't keep on doing what you've been doing, but you can't retire, either."

"So I tried to think what else I could do," he said. "Emmett Dalton wound up in Hollywood, writing movies and dealing in real estate."

"You working on a script, Keller? Boning up for the realtor's exam?"

"I couldn't think of a single thing I could do," he said. "Oh, I suppose I could get some kind of minimum-wage job. But I'm used to living a certain way, and I'm used to not having to work many hours. Can you see me clerking in a 7-Eleven?"

"I couldn't even see you sticking up a 7-Eleven, Keller."

"It might be different if I were younger."

"I guess armed robbery is a young man's job."

"If I were just starting out," he said, "I could take some entry-level job and work my way up. But I'm too old for that now. Nobody would hire me in the first place, and the jobs I'm qualified for, well, I wouldn't want them."

" 'Do you want fries with that?' You're right, Keller. Somehow it just doesn't sound like you."

"I started at the bottom once. I started coming around and the old man found things for me to do. 'Richie's gotta see a man, so why don't you ride along with him, keep him company.' Or go see this guy, tell him we're not happy with the way he's been acting. Or he used to send me to the store to pick up candy bars for him. What was that candy bar he used to like?"

"Mars bars."

"No, he switched to those, but early on it was something else. They were hard to find, only a few stores had them. I think he was the only person I ever met who liked them. What the hell was the name of them? It's on the tip of my tongue."

"Hell of a place for a candy bar."

"Powerhouse," he said. "Powerhouse candy bars."

"The dentist's best friend," she said. "I remember them now. I wonder if they still make them."

" 'Do me a favor, kid, see if they got any of my candy bars downtown.' Then one day it was do me a favor, here's a gun, go see this guy and give him two in the head. Out of the blue, more or less, except by then he probably knew I'd do it. And you know something? It never occurred to me not to. 'Here's a gun, do me a favor.' So I took the gun and did him a favor."

"Just like that?"

"Pretty much. I was used to doing what he told me, and I just did. And that let him know I was somebody who could do that kind of thing. Because not everybody can."

"But it didn't bother you."

"I've been thinking about this," he said. "Reflecting, I guess you'd call it. I didn't let it bother me."

"That thing you do, fading the color out of the image and pushing it off in the distance . . ."

"It was later that I taught myself to do that," he said. "Earlier, well, I guess you'd just call it denial. I told myself it didn't bother me and made myself believe it. And then there was this sense of accomplishment. Look what I did, see what a man I am. Bang, and he's dead and you're not, there's a certain amount of exhilaration that comes with it."

"Still?"

He shook his head. "There's the feeling that you've got the job done, that's all. If it was difficult, well, you've accomplished something. If there are other things you'd rather be doing, well, now you can go home and do them."

"Buy stamps, see a movie."

"Right."

"You just pretended it didn't bother you," she said, "and then one day it didn't."

"And it was easy to pretend, because it never bothered me all that much. But yes, I just kept on doing it, and then I didn't have to pretend. This place I stayed in Scottsdale, there were all these masks on the walls. Tribal stuff, I guess they were. And I thought about how I started out wearing a mask, and before long it wasn't a mask, it was my own face."

"I guess I follow you."

"It's just a way of looking at it," he said. "Anyway, how I got here's not the point. Where do I go from here? That's the question."

"You had a lot of time to think up an answer."

"Too much time."

"I guess, with all the stops in Nashville and Coffee Pot."

"Coffeyville."

"Whatever. What did you come up with, Keller?"

"Well," he said, and drew a breath. "One, I'm ready to stop doing this. The business is different, with the airline security and people living behind stockade fences. And I'm different. I'm older, and I've been doing this for too many years."

"Okay."

"Two, I can't retire. I need the money, and I don't have any other way to earn what I need to live on."

"I hope there's a three, Keller, because one and two don't leave you much room to swing."

"What I had to do," he said, "was figure out how much money I need."

"To retire on."

He nodded. "The figure I came up with," he said, "is a million dollars."

"A nice round sum."

"That's more than I had when I was thinking about retirement the last time. I think this is a more realistic figure. Invested right, I could probably get a return of around fifty thousand dollars a year."

"And you can live on that?"

"I don't want that much," he said. "I'm not thinking in terms of around-the-world cruises and expensive restaurants. I don't spend a lot on clothes, and when I buy something I wear it until it's worn out."

"Or even longer."

"If I had a million in cash," he said, "plus what I could get for the apartment, which is probably another half million."

"Where would you move?"

"I don't know. Someplace warm, I suppose."

"Sundowner Estates?"

"Too expensive. And I wouldn't care to be walled in, and I don't play golf."

"You might, just to have something to do."

He shook his head. "Some of those guys loved golf," he said, "but others, you had the feeling they had to keep selling themselves on the idea, telling each other how crazy they were about the game. 'What time?'"

"How's that?"

"It's the punch line of a joke. It's not important. No, I wouldn't want to live there. But there are these little towns in New Mexico north of Albuquerque, up in the high desert, and you could buy a shack there or just pick up a mobile home and find a place to park it."

"And you think you could stand it? Out in the boonies like that?"

"I don't know. The thing is, say I netted half a million from the apartment, plus the million I saved. Say five percent, comes to seventy-five thousand a year, and yes, I could live fine on that."

"And your apartment's worth half a million?"

"Something like that."

"So all you need is a million dollars, Keller. Now I'd lend it to you, but I'm a little short this month. What are you going to do, sell your stamps?"

"They're not worth anything like that. I don't know what I've spent on the collection, but it certainly doesn't come to a million dollars, and you can't get back what you put into them, anyway."

"I thought they were supposed to be a good investment."

"They're better than spending the money on caviar and champagne," he said, "because you get something back when you sell them, but dealers have to make a profit, too, and if you get half your money back you're doing well. Anyway, I wouldn't want to sell them."

"You want to keep them. And keep on collecting?"

"If I had seventy-five thousand a year coming in," he said, "and if I lived in some little town in the desert, I could afford to spend ten or fifteen thousand a year on stamps."

"I bet northern New Mexico's full of people doing just that."

"Maybe not," he said, "but I don't see why I couldn't do it."

"You could be the first, Keller. Now all you need is a million dollars."

"That's what I was thinking."

"Okay, I'll bite. How're you going to get it?"

"Well," he said, "that pretty much answers itself, doesn't it? I mean, there's only one thing I know how to do."

"I think I get it," Dot said. "You can't do this anymore, so you've got to do it with a vengeance. You have to depopulate half the country in order to get out of the business of killing people."

"When you put it that way . . ."

"Well, there's a certain irony operating, wouldn't you say? But there's a certain logic there, too. You want to grab every high-ticket job that comes along, so that you can salt away enough cash to get out of the business once and for all. You know what it reminds me of?"

"What?"

"Cops," she said. "Their pensions are based on what they make the last year they work, so they grab all the overtime they can get their hands on, and then when they retire they can live in style. Usually we sit back and pick and choose, and you take time off between jobs, but that's not what you want to do now, is it? You want to do a job, come home, catch your breath, then turn around and do another one."

"Right."

"Until you can cash in at an even million."

"That's the idea."

"Or maybe a few dollars more, to allow for inflation."

"Maybe."

"A little more iced tea, Keller?"

"No, I'm fine."

"Would you rather have coffee? I could make coffee."

"No thanks."

"You sure?"

"Positive."

"You took a lot of time in Scottsdale. Did he really look just like the man in Monopoly?"

"In the photo. Less so in real life."

"He didn't give you any trouble?"

He shook his head. "By the time he had a clue what was happening, it was pretty much over."

"He wasn't on his guard at all, then."

"No. I wonder why he got on somebody's list."

"An impatient heir would be my guess. Did it bother you much, Keller? Before, during, or after?"

He thought about it, shook his head.

"And then you took your time getting out of there."

"I thought it made sense to hang around a few days. One more day and I could have gone to the funeral."

"So you left the day they buried him?"

"Except they didn't," he said. "He had the same kind of funeral as Mr. Lattimore."

"Am I supposed to know who that is?"

"He had a house I could have bought. He was cremated, and after a nondenominational service his ashes were placed in the water hazard."

"Just a five-iron shot from his front door."

"Well," Keller said. "Anyway, yes, I took my time getting home."

"All those museums."

"I had to think it all through," he said. "Figuring out what I want to do with the rest of my life."

"Of which today is the first day, if I remember correctly. Let me make sure I've got this straight. You're done feeding rescue workers at Ground Zero, and you're done going to museums for dead outlaws, and you're ready to get out there and kill one for the Gipper. Is that about it?"

"It's close enough."

"Because I've been turning down jobs left and right, Keller, and what I want to do is get on the horn and spread the word that we're ready to do business. We're not holding any two-for-one sales, but we're very much in the game. Am I clear on that?" She got to her feet. "Which reminds me. Don't go away."

She came back with an envelope and dropped it on the table in front of him. "They paid up right away, and it took you so long to get home I was beginning to think of it as my money. What's this?"

"Something I picked up on the way home."

She opened the package, took the little black clay pot in her hands. "That's really nice," she said. "What is it, Indian?"

"From a pueblo in New Mexico."

"And it's for me?"

"I got the urge to buy it," he said, "and then afterward I wondered what I was going to do with it. And I thought maybe you'd like it."

"It would look nice on the mantel," she said. "Or it would be handy to keep paperclips in. But it'll have to be one or the other, because there's no point in keeping paperclips on the mantel. You said you got it in New Mexico? In the town you're figuring to wind up in?"

He shook his head. "It was a pueblo. I think you have to be an Indian."

"Well, they do nice work. I'm very pleased to have it."

"Glad you like it."

"And you take good care of that," she said, pushing the envelope toward him. "It's the first deposit in your retirement fund. Though I suppose you'll want to spend some of it on stamps."

Two days later he was working on his stamps when the phone rang. "I'm in the city," she said. "Right around the corner from you, as a matter of fact."

She told him the name of the restaurant, and he went there and found her in a booth at the back, eating an ice cream sundae. "When I was a kid," she said, "they had these at Wohler's drugstore for thirty-five cents. It was five cents extra if you wanted walnuts on top. I'd hate to tell you what they get for this beauty, and walnuts weren't part of the deal, either."

"Nothing's the way it used to be."

"You're right about that," she said, "and a philosophical observation like that is worth the trip. But it's not why I came in. Here's the waitress, Keller. You want one of these?"

He shook his head, ordered a cup of coffee. The waitress brought it, and when she was out of earshot Dot said, "I had a call this morning."

"Oh?"

"And I was going to call you, but it wasn't anything to discuss on the phone, and I didn't feel right about telling you to come out to White Plains because I was pretty sure you'd be wasting your time. So I figured I'd come in, and have an ice cream sundae while I'm at it. It's worth the trip, incidentally, even if they do charge the earth for it. You sure you don't want one?"

"Positive."

"I got a call," she said, "from a guy we've worked with before, a broker, very solid type. And there's some work to be done, a nice upscale piece of work, which would put a nice piece of change in your retirement fund and one in mine, too."

"What's the catch?"

"It's in Santa Barbara, California," she said, "and there's a very narrow window operating. You'd have to do it Wednesday or Thursday, which makes it impossible, because it would take longer than that for you to drive there even if you left right away and only stopped for gas. I mean, suppose you drove it in three days, which is ridiculous anyway. You'd be wiped out when you got there, and you'd get there when, Thursday afternoon at the earliest? Can't be done."

"No."

"So I'll tell them no," she said, "but I wanted to check with you first."

"Tell them we'll do it," he said.

"Really?"

"I'll fly out tomorrow morning. Or tonight, if I can get something."

"You weren't ever going to fly again."

"I know."

"And then a job comes along . . ."

"Not flying just doesn't seem that important," he said. "Don't ask me why."

"Actually," she said, "I have a theory."

"Oh?"

"When the Towers came down," she said, "it was very traumatic for you. Same as it was for everybody else. You had to adjust to a new reality, and that's not easy to do. Your whole world went tilt, and for a while there you stayed off airplanes, and you went downtown and fed the hungry, and you bided your time and tried to figure out a way to get along without doing your usual line of work."

"And?"

"And time passed," she said, "and things settled down, and you adjusted to the way the world is now. While you were at it, you realized what you'll have to do if you're going to be in a position to retire. You thought things through and came up with a plan."

"Well, sort of a plan."

"And a lot of things which seemed very important a while ago, like not flying with all this security and ID checks and all, turn out to be just an inconvenience and not something to make you change your life around. You'll get a second set of ID, or you'll use real ID and find some other way to cover your tracks. One way or another, you'll work it out."

"I suppose," he said. "Santa Barbara. That's between L.A. and San Francisco, isn't it?"

"Closer to L.A. They have their own airport."

He shook his head. "They can keep it," he said. "I'll fly to LAX. Or Burbank, that's even better, and I'll rent a car and drive up to Santa Barbara. Wednesday or Thursday, you said?" He pressed his wrists together. " 'What time?' "

"What time? What do you mean, what time? What's so funny, anyway?"

"Oh, it's a joke one of the golfers told in the clubhouse in Scottsdale. This golfer goes out and he has the worst round of his life. He loses balls in the rough, he can't get out of sand traps, he hits ball after ball into the water hazard. Nothing goes right for him. By the time he gets to the eighteenth green all he's got left is his putter, because he's broken every other club over his knee, and after he fourputts the final hole he breaks the putter, too, and sends it flying.

"He marches into the locker room, absolutely furious, and he unlocks his locker and takes out his razor and opens it up and gets the blade in his hand and slashes both his wrists. And he stands there, watching the blood flow, and someone calls to him over the bank of lockers. 'Hey, Joe,' the guy says, 'we're getting up a foursome for tomorrow morning. You interested?' "

"And the guy says"—Keller raised his hands to shoulder height, pressed his wrists together—" 'What time?' "

" 'What time?' "

"Right."

" 'What time?' " She shook her head. "I like it, Keller. And any old time you want'll be just fine."